"I think you're wildly attracted to me and don't know what to do about it?"

"Wildly attracted?" Liz raised one eyebrow. "At one time, I might have been very attracted to you, Mitch McCoy...." She paused and looked him in the eye. "But now I wouldn't even consider..."

"Sleeping with me?"

"You already missed your opportunity there. From here on out, something like that will only happen in your dreams."

Mitch nodded. "Yep, there too." He shook his head. "Only, I know for sure I'm not dreaming now. Because if I were, the diner would be empty. And you wouldn't be standing there wearing that uniform, no matter how cute you look in it."

"Oh, and where would I be?" she countered.

He gave her a sexy grin. "For starters, you'd be stretched across this counter, with those long legs of yours..."

Liz took a step back, her pulse leaping. "That's enough. I think I got the picture."

"But darli o the part abo

D0967118

Dear Reader,

Ask and you shall receive. When we wrote *License To Thrill*, the first book in THE MAGNIFICENT McCOY MEN miniseries, we were overwhelmed with requests for more stories about Marc and his sexy-as-sin brothers. So how could we resist?

In *The P.I. Who Loved Her*, restless Mitch McCoy comes face-to-face with his former fiancée, Liz Braden, on the side of a dark country road. Not only did Liz leave him at the altar seven years ago, but the wedding dress she's wearing tells him she's just left another poor fool in the same situation. Mitch's dilemma: keeping his hands off the only woman he's ever wanted—long enough to figure out what, or who, she's running from.

We hope you enjoy watching Liz lead Mitch on a merry little dance that ends up where it should have seven years ago—in the bedroom! We'd love to hear what you think. Write to us at P.O. Box 12271, Toledo, OH 43612, or visit us at the web site we share with other Temptation authors at Temptationauthors.com. And be sure to keep your eyes peeled for the next MAGNIFICENT McCOY coming your way....

Here's wishing you many happy endings,

Lori and Tony Karayianni
aka Tori Carrington

Books by Tori Carrington

HARLEQUIN TEMPTATION
716—CONSTANT CRAVING
740—LICENSE TO THRILL

THE P.I. WHO LOVED HER
Tori Carrington

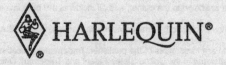

HARLEQUIN®

TORONTO • NEW YORK • LONDON
AMSTERDAM • PARIS • SYDNEY • HAMBURG
STOCKHOLM • ATHENS • TOKYO • MILAN • MADRID
PRAGUE • WARSAW • BUDAPEST • AUCKLAND

We lovingly dedicate this book to the memory of our fathers,
Carl J. Schlachter and Vagelis Karayianni,
two men who showed us what being a true hero is all about.
And to Kostoula Karayianni, a woman who would make
any heroine envious.

And last but not least, here's a hearty thank-you
to Brenda Chin and Birgit Davis-Todd.
You two not only make it possible for us to do what we love;
you make us love what we do.

ISBN 0-373-25876-3

THE P.I. WHO LOVED HER

Copyright © 2000 by Lori and Tony Karayianni.

1

"YOU KNOW, Mitch McCoy, you really need to get a life."

Mitch downshifted as he neared the outskirts of Manchester County, Virginia, then tugged at his tie. Only the pickup's headlights broke the inky darkness, his own voice broke the all-consuming silence. Still, he wouldn't be surprised if Sheriff Mathison waited on the other side of the next cornfield, ready to nab him for speeding. Next to him, Goliath stared at the closed passenger window, a patch of coffee-colored fur disturbed by the air conditioner blower. The dog—a mammoth, butt-ugly husky and shepherd mix—whined and turned mournful eyes on him.

"I know what you mean, sport. I know what you mean."

And he did know. In the past few months he'd come to know exactly what wanting an unnamed something meant. Waking up in the morning in a cold sweat, reaching for something—or someone—that wasn't there. Speaking thoughts and ideas aloud only to discover there was no one around to hear. Living with an intangible hole in the vicinity of his chest—a hole that wasn't going to be filled tonight by going home to an empty house.

The entire McCoy clan was still in Bedford, Maryland, celebrating his brother Marc's marriage to Melanie Weber, even though the miserably happy couple had already left for their honeymoon cruise to the U.S. Virgin Islands. *The Virgin Islands.* Marc had said something about it being romantic. Maybe it was Marc and Mel's idea of romance. A ship would be the last place he'd find romantic. All that…water. Garish tropical-print shirts. Food-laden buffet tables. Sunshine. Sex—

Mitch's foot slipped from the gas pedal. Where had *that* thought come from?

It wasn't that he begrudged his brother his happiness. It was a miracle Marc and Mel had finally sorted everything out, despite the drastic way in which they had. It was just that, of the five McCoy siblings, clueless Marc seemed like the last person who would stand at an altar, much less be the first.

Well, he hadn't exactly been the *first*. But he had been the first to actually make it to the nuptials part.

That was it—the reason he was so agitated. All this talk of weddings…of the L word…of making promises and sticking to them. It should have occurred to him when he'd had to squirm in that uncomfortable pew for an hour, forced to watch Marc and Melanie complete what he had never had. Forced to remember the day he'd been left at the altar as if it were yesterday.

But it hadn't been yesterday. He tugged at his tie again. It was seven years ago last month Liz Braden had left the town, and him, behind.

At any rate, his…restlessness hadn't developed overnight. No, it had been months—if not years—in the making. He'd grown listless in his role as P.I., just as years before he'd grown frustrated at the rigmarole as an FBI agent. While he still shared an office in D.C. with his two partners, Mike Schaffer and Renee Delancy, he'd passed most of his clients over to them, keeping only those to whom he felt personally obligated. Then he'd returned home to Manchester to pursue a dusty old dream—a dream he'd secretly harbored since his mother had told him about the Connor tradition of horse-breeding. He'd readily abandoned the fantasy at eighteen when he'd followed in the footsteps of every other McCoy male for the past four generations and entered the military, then later, law enforcement.

But rather than his frustration abating as a result of the recent changes in his life, it had quadrupled. The crappy thing was he knew exactly when that had happened: the night Marc had asked him about Liz Braden.

What was it his brother had asked? He couldn't remember the exact words, but he all too clearly remembered their meaning: Had he ever regretted not going after Liz?

If only Marc knew that he *had* gone after her. In a sense, anyway.

Goliath whined again, louder this time. Mitch frowned at him in the darkness. "What is it, G? Do you have to water the weeds?"

The mutt lumbered to an alert position, a line of slobber dropping from the side of his meaty mouth to his elephantine front paws, indented on the edge of the seat.

Mitch glanced in the rearview mirror to find the road behind him empty. He downshifted again and flicked on his high beams, illuminating the dark stretch of Route 28 in front of him.

Aw, who was he kidding? He was the last person to be applying armchair psychology to his life. In all likelihood, his agitated state was due to something far simpler. Say, lack of sex? It had been a long time since he'd buried himself in some prime, sleek, female flesh. Too long. He told himself that right now any female would do. But he knew that wasn't true. He simply figured that's how most men who hadn't had any in awhile feel.

Fifty feet ahead on the opposite side of the two-lane road, a stopped car with its yellow hazard lights flashing stood out against the otherwise black June night.

Still, someone with a great smile and a fine pair of thighs

would be nice. He squinted at the woman standing next to the car. Anyone but—

Liz.

Mitch tightly hauled the steering wheel to the left to stop the truck from catapulting over the embankment and into the ditch. He cursed, his heart rate leaping. Marc and his damn questions. He'd never have thought of Liz if it wasn't for his brother. Well, that wasn't entirely true, but he'd certainly never hallucinated seeing her before.

He was worse off than he thought.

A deep breath whistled from between his teeth as he stared at the brand-spanking-new Lexus gleaming in the twin beams of his headlights. In a town filled with pickups, a pricey automobile pulled off the side of the road at twelve-thirty in the morning was sure to raise some speculation. Goliath nudged his shoulder. Mitch ignored him as the bright beam of his headlights reflected off the woman kneeling next to the left rear tire.

His brakes quietly squealed as he stopped his truck even with the car. "Need some help, lady?"

The woman wrenched a crowbar up and down. Mitch's gaze followed the way her sweetly shaped bottom within her white dress swayed with each movement. Hmmm....

"Thanks, but no," she said. "I've changed tires before. One more isn't going to make much of a difference."

Mitch glanced at the digital clock on his dash, then back to her tempting backside. To hell with wanting someone with a great smile. He'd settle for a grade-A bottom like this one had.

It's a wedding dress.

He stared at the silky white material skimming the woman's lavish curves and nearly choked. Okay, that was it. He'd had enough of weddings, and anything associated with them, to last a lifetime.

Goliath pawed his denim-clad legs. Mitch held the dog back from where he strained toward the open window.

"What's up, G?" He hadn't seen him this animated in years. The tinny sound of music reached his ears. It wafted from the open door of the Lexus. Country, he guessed, grimacing. He scanned the lighted interior, finding the car empty. No air freshener hanging from the mirror, no purse on the seat, no sign of a suitcase or overnight bag. He glanced over the roof toward the dark ditch he knew paralleled the road. He found no sign of a shadowy figure waiting to ambush him.

"You're getting cynical in your old age," he muttered, then said to her, "Suit yourself."

He shifted the truck back into gear.

He'd moved thirty feet before he stepped on the brakes again. He tapped his side-view mirror until the woman in white was back in sight. *Damn.* He couldn't just leave her there. Despite his natural caution and the fact that the county crime rate was basically nil, Pops had taught him and his brothers better than to leave anyone—much less a woman—stranded on the road in the middle of the night.

Sighing, Mitch hooked a U-turn, bringing his truck back behind the Lexus and its Massachusetts license plate. Nothing to indicate it was a rental. Then again, most states had done away with marking rentals. He ground to a stop directly behind the car. He rolled up the window enough to prevent Goliath from jumping out, then climbed from the truck cab.

"Indulge me," he said, before she could protest. He hoisted the spare from the Lexus's trunk, then nudged her out of the way. "Neither of us is going to rest until you're safely back on the road." He jacked the car up a little higher, his muscles bunching under his shirt at the familiar scent of wild cherries. The music battled with the cadence of crickets in a nearby cornfield.

"Mitch?" the woman said over the sound of a twangy guitar. "Mitch McCoy, is that you?"

He stood up so quickly, he nearly tripped over the spare lying on the road behind him.

Holy... It *was* Liz.

WELL I'LL BE....

Liz dragged her gaze over the long, delicious length of man standing before her, from his shiny boots, to his tight, new jeans, then up to where a tie hung haphazardly around the collar of his crisp white shirt. She didn't know who was more shocked by the midnight encounter, her or Mitch. And she was definitely sure the fine specimen before her was Mitch. Years may have passed since she'd last seen him, but she'd recognize the tantalizing man anywhere. No one could fill out a pair of jeans quite the way Mitch could.

Liz ran the tip of her tongue along her suddenly dry lips. *Amazing.*

She finally looked up to his face and gave a short, impulsive laugh. No, she'd have to say *he* was the more surprised of the two by far. He looked like someone had just whacked him in the head with a two-by-four. She smiled. Imagine that. She had rendered Mitch McCoy speechless.

"You changed your hair color," he finally blurted, more than said.

She tucked a dark strand behind her ear, a small part of her flattered he'd noticed—which was majorly stupid. The last thing she should have been doing was blushing at a man's attentions. Even if that man was Mitch McCoy. "Yeah. I, um, didn't always have more fun as a blonde." Of course, she wasn't having that much fun as a brunette either, if her current predicament was any indication.

His gaze flicked rather than slid over her attire, lingering in certain places and causing a curious, sizzling warmth to meander through her bloodstream. Well, *that* certainly hadn't changed, had it? It had taken Richard Beschloss five dates to get to first base with her. One look from Mitch and...

Well, she didn't think it prudent to take that thought any further.

His gaze reached her breasts. The meandering heat quickened to a scamper and she found it suddenly impossible to breathe.

His gaze quickly lifted to her face. "Liz, is that blood on your dress? What kind of trouble have you gotten yourself into now?"

If anything was capable of reminding her of the mess she was currently in, *that* was. She glanced down at the dark stain on the bright white of her dress. Trust Mitch to immediately identify it correctly. Back in Jersey she'd gotten away with telling a gas station attendant she'd spilled chocolate syrup on herself.

She looked back at Mitch, whose gaze was riveted to her breasts.

"Are you hurt?" he asked.

"No...no, I'm fine," she said, feeling the ridiculous urge to laugh again. Now her ex-groom, on the other hand.... "Don't, um, worry, it's not mine. I'm as fit as the day I last saw you."

Mitch reached up and tugged almost violently on his tie, drawing her gaze to the base of his neck. All at once, her mind filled with the image of the two of them standing in the front room of Gran's house, him in his new suit, her standing in her bare feet staring at him proudly. It had been his first official day as an agent of the FBI. "Why, Mitch McCoy, you clean up real nice." She'd laid on her best southern drawl, forgetting how torn she was between wanting him to succeed in what he'd chosen to do, and needing him to be there for her.

How long had it taken her to break him of the habit of fussing with his tie? Two months? Three? How many times had she smoothed his collar, only to be sidetracked by the clean-smelling expanse of his skin there, just under his jaw?

She dragged her gaze up to his, watching her guardedly. She caught her bottom lip between her teeth.

"Somehow I knew you'd still be in Manchester," she said, her voice a little too breathless, a little too revealing. She reached for the crowbar and continued jacking up the car. "Small-town boy Mitch McCoy, who'll die in the same spot he was born."

She slid a glance over her shoulder, relieved to find him grimacing at the jibe. "What's *that* supposed to mean?"

She shrugged.

Oh, yeah, she'd known odds were she'd run into Mitch when she came back to Manchester. And she'd even admit to feeling a tingle of excitement at the prospect of coming face-to-face with him. The only problem was, she hadn't counted on running into him the instant she rolled over the county line. Hadn't expected to be reminded of how much she had missed him.

That was just one of those things about life: when it rained, it bloody well stormed.

She cleared her throat. "How's, um, your father?" she asked, acutely aware that he was watching her backside.

He jostled her out of the way then knelt in front of the tire. "Fine. He's fine."

"And your brothers?"

"They're fine, too." He sat back on his heels. "Look, Liz, I'm really not in the mood for a game of catch-up. It's been a really long day. I'd like nothing more than to get you on your way, then go home and crawl into bed." She watched him stiffen, then close his eyes and mutter a curse. He finished hoisting the car up and methodically removed the lug nuts from the flat. Her mind turned over all the possible reasons for his reaction, then she homed in on the most likely: the mention of bed and her in the same sentence.

The warmth that had spread through her veins earlier edged up a degree or two. She rode out a delicious shiver, and tried to remind herself of the long list of reasons she had *not* to play with the fire flickering in front of her in the shape of Mitch McCoy. First and foremost, the fact that she had been minutes away from marrying another man, oh, not twelve hours ago.

Still, not even that impetus was enough to stop her from wanting Mitch in much the same way she'd always wanted him, despite the number of years that separated then from now.

He glanced at her over a broad shoulder. "So what brings you back to Manchester, Liz? Last I heard, you were in Chicago."

She smiled. He might not want to play catch-up when it came to himself, but it appeared she was a whole different matter. "So you kept tabs on me. I'm impressed." She watched his frown deepen. "I do have to say I'm a little disappointed, though. I left Chicago a few years back."

"Let me guess. You left for Massachusetts."

"Um, actually no," she said quietly. "There were a couple of cities in between." She felt inexplicably uncomfortable. "But they don't matter. Not now."

The crowbar slipped from a lug nut and he nearly pierced the flat tire with the pointed end.

"What is it with the dress, Liz? Is your groom stashed in the trunk, or is this style one you've taken a liking to?"

She inwardly winced at the below-the-belt jab. "I don't

know, Mitch. Did you see anyone in the trunk when you got the tire out?"

"Damn. Stepped right into that one, didn't I?" He continued working on the flat tire. "You never answered my question."

She stared at him blankly.

"What are you doing back in Manchester?"

Now that *was* a question. What was she doing back in Manchester? It was something she'd been asking herself ever since she realized a few hours ago that was where she was heading.

She shrugged. "I don't know. I was feeling a little nostalgic for the past, maybe?" She turned away from where he watched her a little too closely and drew in a deep breath of the damp, summer night air. "I'll be on my way as soon as some things settle down in Boston."

She hadn't realized he'd moved until he stood right next to her. "These things that need to settle down—they don't have anything to do with the blood on your dress, do they?"

She glanced at Mitch's profile in the darkness. For just an instant, she remembered that her favorite pastime had once been staring at him. Tracing the outline of his nose with her finger...running her tongue along the fine ridge of his jaw....

She cleared her throat. "No. Well, not exactly anyway." She wiped at a smudge on her long skirt then turned her best smile on him. "This stain really has you worked up, doesn't it?"

He rubbed his long, slender fingers against his chin, making her fingers ache to do the same. "Yeah, well, you always did have this way of getting under my skin."

"Yeah. Ditto," she said, eyeing his mouth. His wide, generous mouth she had once kissed for hours at a stretch. Dipping her tongue in and out of its hot wetness. Sucking on his bottom lip then catching it between her teeth. "Guess some things never change, no matter how much you want them to."

"Yeah."

Her gaze slammed into his. What seemed like an eternity of unanswered questions and unacknowledged truths seemed to pass between them. Then Mitch drew away and moved stiffly back to the car, a line of quiet oaths filling his wake.

Liz straightened the strap of her dress and sighed. Truth be told, she didn't know what she was doing back in Manchester. One minute she was punching Richard in the nose at the Beschloss estate, the next she was on her way to Virginia with no clothes, no resources, and every reason to think she wouldn't have access to either for awhile. At least not until Rich regained his cool. Of course, if she'd known what was going to happen, she never would have sold her apartment and moved all her things to Rich's place. Or rushed out with little more than her car keys and the clothes on her back, her plans not stretching beyond getting out of the house *now*. Good thing she always kept her driver's license and a gas card in the car's glove compartment or she'd never have made it out of Massachusetts. She'd also found a few dollars' worth of change in the car, but that was it.

She had suspected there was something inherently wrong with getting engaged to a spoiled bank vice president whose family just happened to own the financial institution he worked at and where she had all her accounts. And here she thought her misgivings had to do with all that blue blood that ran through his veins.

Then there was Mitch....

She watched him lower the car and tighten the lug nuts. He got up and held out the crowbar and jack.

"Here. Since you didn't want my help to begin with, I'm sure you won't mind cleaning up."

She accepted the items, then flicked a glance down the road. Mitch followed her line of vision.

"What's the matter? You expecting company?"

She laughed her response, then abruptly stopped. Was it naive to think that Rich wouldn't follow her?

The sound of a barking dog made her jump. Then she recognized the over-zealous, roaring bark of this particular dog. She stared at the truck behind the Lexus.

"That's not..." She met Mitch's exasperated gaze. "You still have Goliath?"

His silence was all the answer she needed. She thrust the jack and crowbar back at him, then lifted her skirts and hurried in the direction of the truck.

Mitch stood planted to the spot on the asphalt, clutching the tools. He felt as if someone had grabbed the edges of the invisible rug that constituted his life and given it a good yank, throwing everything into chaos. Funny, it was the same way he had always felt when around Liz Braden. Actually, it depended on the day. Years ago he'd described her as the sunlight that had chased the shadows from the dark side of his soul. Tonight, she was definitely a rug-yanker.

He watched her open the truck door as enthusiastically as if she wore jeans and a T-shirt rather than a wedding dress. The aging brown-white-and-black dappled dog leapt out. If he didn't know better, he would think the mutt recognized the woman who had rescued him from life as a mangy farm dog. He lapped repeatedly at her face and ran around her with more energy than he'd shown for years. Remembering Goliath's whining in the truck before he'd even spotted the disabled car, he idly wondered if the dog had known what was coming all along.

Or maybe he was as much of a sucker for a pretty face as he was.

Mitch leaned against the bed of the truck, watching the

two get reacquainted, Liz murmuring endearments and roughhousing with a dog he would have thought she'd forgotten by now. Forgotten much as she had forgotten him.

"God, how old is he?" she asked.

"Twelve." Mitch cast a glance down the dark road. What had she been looking for?

"Don't worry," she said, stepping beside him, a puppy-like Goliath at her heels. "I lost the car following me a couple hundred miles back."

"Car?" Mitch jerked toward her. "What car?"

"I'm joking. Like I said, there's nothing to worry about." He noted the teasing look in her eyes. "What are you doing out this late, anyway?"

"I...it's..." he started, then stopped, the irony of the situation just now hitting him. "I'm coming back from a wedding reception in Maryland." He tugged again at his tie. "Marc got married."

She nodded, the warm silence of the night pressing in around Mitch along with the pure scent of her. "And you?" she asked.

"Me what?"

She motioned toward his tie and dress attire. "Are you...married?"

He made a point of slowly gazing at her dress. The bloodstain was limited to the one area. No splatters, not a trace on the long, lacy skirt. "Yep. Five years. Three kids. Five cats. A goat. All complete with white picket fence."

Her eyes narrowed. He grinned.

"I'm joking," he said, echoing her words of moments before. Hey, two could play at this game, couldn't they? "Nope, I'm not married. One try at the altar was enough for me."

"Cute. Really cute, McCoy." She laughed. "Funny, I just realized the same thing about myself this morning. About one try at the altar, that is." Her hazel eyes twinkled in a way that made it impossible to look away.

In that moment, it was almost too easy to forget she had once run her hand lovingly down his chest only to rip his heart out. Her gaze said as much as it ever had...maybe even more. Her luscious mouth just as little.

Concentrate on the bloodstain, McCoy. The bloodstain.

"Well, I guess I'd better get back on the road," she said. "There's a lot I have to do before I call it a night."

Mitch squashed the urge to grasp her wrist, to ask her exactly what she had to do, where she had been, why she had changed the color of her hair...anything to make her stay a little longer.

His reaction surprised even him.

But rather than giving in to it, he pulled in a deep breath, then let loose a sharp whistle. Goliath loped back from the long grass at the side of the road. The dog burrowed his nose into Liz's wedding dress and whined, then bounded into the truck.

"You staying at your grandmother's place?" he asked, thinking of the old Victorian that hunkered at the edge of town. Though Old Man Peabody looked after it, no one had lived there since Liz's maternal grandmother had died, and Liz herself had left seven years ago for parts unknown.

"I was thinking about it."

He hiked an eyebrow. "Aren't you going in the wrong direction?"

She shivered visibly despite the warm air. "I...I thought I'd take a look around town and see what's changed first. You know, this being my first time back in so long."

He nodded as if the idea made perfect sense. It made none. What was she hoping to see at twelve-thirty in the morning? He looked back down the road. "Well, I probably won't be crossing paths with you again before you leave. Have a nice visit, won't you?"

Tucking her wayward white skirt around her legs, she climbed into the Lexus. He closed the door for her, but not before he caught a glimpse of her spike-heeled red shoes. He jammed his fingers through his hair.

"Goodbye, Mitch," she said through the open window.

"Right, 'bye."

He stepped back from the door to allow her to drive away. He should be getting into his truck, heading for the empty McCoy farmhouse a couple of miles away. But he stood stock-still, his gaze plastered to the rear end of the Lexus. He barely noticed the hazard lights were still flashing. His entire body pounded with lust. Lust remembered and re-ignited.

Liz was back.

LIZ MISSED the turnoff by half a car length, backed up, then pulled the Lexus onto the two ruts that served as her grandmother's driveway. She coasted rather than pulled to a stop, then put the car in Park.

She lay back against the buttery leather headrest, surprised to find herself feeling more than a bit...well, flighty. The sensation had begun the instant she realized she couldn't marry Richard and had climbed to dizzying proportions when she'd bumped into Mitch. If she were a believer in cosmic events, fate, she might even indulge in a little wagering that a higher being had masterminded the entire midnight meeting by guaranteeing that her tire would go flat at just the moment Mitch was passing by.

Except that she had noticed the tire was losing air somewhere back in Jersey. She had thought about changing it then, but once she'd realized where she was heading, she'd been in an all-fired hurry to get there. She'd stopped only for gas.

Still, the tire could have waited until she got to Gran's.....

Blaming her errant thoughts on lack of sleep and the sharp change of direction her life had taken, she automatically reached for a purse that wasn't there, then opened the car door. It wasn't until she was halfway to the back of the house that she noticed the hazard lights were still blinking. She didn't care. She was too busy reacquainting herself with the familiar structure in the dim beams of the headlights.

How many summers had she spent here when she was growing up? Ten? Twelve? Regardless of the number, it struck her that the old house was the singular constant in her life, a place that remained the same while the rest of her surroundings forever changed. This house and her grandmother had been an anchor in a world made topsy-turvy, first, by her mother's perpetual migrating from city to city, apartment to apartment, then, by her own almost vagabond existence. When she was younger, Liz had always known she could handle anything as long as she could share those brief, sweet summer months with Gran. It was the place she had run to now.

Her steps slowed the nearer she drew to the back door. Unlike years before, though, Gran wouldn't be there waiting for her, to hug her in that suffocating way that always made her smile, question her about her new haircut, or tell her those goofy stories to illuminate the reasons why she shouldn't grow up too soon.

Boy, could she really use a wise-up talk from Gran now.

But she had lost Minerva Braden seven years ago...she had inherited all that had been hers...become engaged to Mitch, then...

"That was all a long, long time ago, Lizzie," she said out loud, using the words she imagined her grandmother would have. "Before Mitch. Before that jerk Richard Beschloss. Before you found yourself on the road with no purse, no clothes, nowhere to go...."

Despite the dark, she knew exactly where to put her hand over the window molding to find the back-door key. She was glad Old Man Peabody hadn't moved it during his weekly checks and maintenance of the place. She remembered asking Gran once why she bothered even locking the door if everyone knew where the key was anyway. Her grandmother had told her that if someone was that determined to get in, let them do it in a way that wouldn't require repairs. Liz wrapped her fingers around the cool metal, then inserted the key in the lock, bombarded by memories of Gran's practical wisdom.

Assaulted, as well, by sexy memories of Mitch McCoy.

Yes, she admitted, she'd frequently revisited memories of her first love during her time away. Memories that had seen her through some particularly lonely stretches. Memories that had grown tattered with time, but, in one midnight meeting, had grown vividly...real all over again.

Before she'd even completely closed the door, she kicked off her red shoes in the mudroom, then she started stripping out of the constraining wedding dress. She sucked in her breath and yanked down the zipper as she made her way into the kitchen and across the room to where she knew a kerosene lamp was stored in the pantry. She pulled the top of the dress down over her camisole, and freed her arms, feeling around on the second shelf as she shimmied out of the dress. Taking the lamp down, its weight and the sloshing of the kerosene making her sigh in relief, she picked up the dress and strode toward the counter where she found matches in a top drawer.

Within moments the room was aglow with warm light...enough light for her to examine just how bad the stain on the front of the wedding dress was. She bit her bottom lip. It was much worse than she thought. No wonder Mitch had asked so many questions. She couldn't blame him for thinking she'd offed someone. It looked suspiciously as if she had.

Who'd have thought so much blood could gush out of a person's nose?

Once on the road, she had stopped at the first gas station, then gone into the bathroom to pour some water over the dress. Given that the mirror had been little more than a scratchy piece of metal, she hadn't been able to get a good look at the damage. What she could see now made her cringe to think what it would look like in daylight.

It was a shame really. She'd liked the dress. In fact, she'd liked the dress more than she'd liked the man she had almost married. But that revelation hadn't come until just before the ceremony, when she realized she couldn't marry a man she didn't love.

I should have just run out on him like I ran out on Mitch.

She poked the tip of her finger into a loop in the intricate lace. The reason she had sought Richard out was she hadn't wanted to do to another man what she had done to Mitch McCoy.

Foot by foot, she piled the dress up onto the counter, catching it twice when it would have slithered over the side, then picked up the lamp and went in search of something to wear.

Funny, the tricks the mind plays on a person. In her heart, Mitch was still that dreamy-eyed, strapping twenty-five-year-old. Who would have thought he would have...filled out so nicely? Her stocking feet padding against the dusty wood floor, she made her way up the stairs. His green eyes seemed somehow more intense with the slight crinkles at the corners. His hair was longer than the short cut he'd worn then, nearly brushing the tops of his shoulders in a wild way that made her remember back when they had played cowboys and Indians in Farmer Howard's bean fields. Mitch had always played the Indian—a Mohawk more accurately, because he'd always been the exacting type—while she had taken great joy in wearing a gunbelt and squeezing off the caps trailing from the toy metal gun.

But that part hadn't been the most fun. Oh, no, the best part was when they sat down to hammer out the details of their peace treaty, which ultimately led to playful romps on the sun-warmed ground.

She caught herself smiling...again. She hadn't smiled this much—genuinely smiled—in what seemed like forever. She and Mitch had been a whole eight and eleven then. Not that it mattered. For some reason, they'd always fit well. Even Gran had mentioned it...years later, right after she had tanned Liz's hide after a particularly explorative roll in Old Man Peabody's cornfields with Mitch that left her with her shirt unbuttoned, her budding, sensitive chest exposed to the hot summer sun.

At the top of the stairs, Liz stopped and leaned against the railing. She didn't think it odd that she was remembering all this now...and enjoying it. As far as her professional life was concerned—along with her personal life on top of that—she had just suffered one hell of a setback. If Richard froze her assets as he'd threatened, she was facing a major demotion. From top-paid business consultant to homeless person, overnight.

Talk about setbacks.

Still, she couldn't seem to make herself care one way or another right now. Though she did need to figure out a way to get her hands on some cash at some point soon.

She stumbled toward her old bedroom—once her mother's room, with little cabbage roses on the wallpaper and a canopy bed. She put the lamp on the side table and listlessly scavenged through the bureau drawers. She took her old pillow out, then opened the next one. The plastic covering the one item that lay at the bottom of the cavernous depths seemed to wink at her. She reached in and touched her old waitressing uniform. It seemed so very long ago when she'd worked at Bo and Ruth's Paradise Diner.

Smiling wistfully, she stripped the cover sheet from the bare mattress. Sleep. That's what she needed. She was too bushed to think about Rich and all the havoc he'd promised to wreak. Too exhausted to wonder about her meandering visits to the past, and her body-thrumming reaction to Mitch McCoy. Too tired to hunt for something else to wear, to take off her lingerie or to get linens from the hall closet. Tomorrow was soon enough to do all that and to try to make some kind of sense out of the mess that was her life.

2

MITCH HAD NO SOONER closed his eyes than they were wide open again. He rolled over...and nearly injured himself for life. Lying flat on his back, he groaned at his fully aroused state and tried to rid his mind of the images even now clinging to the edges of his consciousness. Provocative lips... tantalizing curves...the flick of a pink tongue. All belonging to one woman: Liz.

So much for getting any sleep.

He got up from the bed and yanked up his shade to find the sun peeking over the mist-shrouded horizon. He grimaced. Despite his exhausted state, he must have squeezed out a few hours of shut-eye, because it was morning already.

He headed for the bathroom, took a bracing, cold shower, dressed, then headed down to the kitchen. He stopped in the empty room. Where the hell was Pops?

He wasn't sure what he was looking for. A return to normalcy, maybe? A solid sign that his life hadn't completely gone to hell in a handbasket overnight? Perhaps he wanted to tell his father Liz had returned and get some of that advice Pops had been real good at doling out lately? It occurred to him that he hadn't heard Sean come in from Maryland last night.

He started the coffee, then headed toward the foot of the stairs. "Pops? Coffee's on!"

He glanced at his watch. It wasn't like his father not to be up yet. Sundays he usually beat the sun and had breakfast half fixed by the time Mitch even thought about crawling out of bed. It was the one morning they spent together by mutual, silent agreement, before Mitch headed out to tick off the next item on his list of things-to-be-done around the property and before Sean went off to...

He scratched his head, only then realizing he had no idea what his dad had been doing with his Sundays lately.

"Pops? You want eggs or pancakes for breakfast?"

"Eggs sound good."

Mitch swung around to face his father coming in from outside. He shrugged out of his suit coat. His *suit coat*. It suddenly dawned on him that he hadn't heard his dad come in last night because he never *had* come in.

"Hey, Mitch, I see you made it home all right."

Mitch watched him pour a cup of coffee. "Yeah, good thing one of us did."

Sean took a long sip, his face a little too...cheerful for Mitch's liking. "Yeah" was all he said, then grinned.

Mitch grimaced.

Okay, chances were that his dad had had one too many at Marc and Mel's wedding reception and had opted for a motel room rather than making the long ride home. Or...

He groaned. Or else Pops's sex life was a whole helluva lot more active than his.

He rubbed his forehead. He couldn't remember a time when he could link the words "Pops" and "sex" together. He wasn't sure how he felt about his ability to do so now. From what he remembered, and what others had to say in the small, everybody-knows-everybody-else's-business town, Pops had been blown away by his wife's unexpected death. While it didn't completely excuse some of the rougher periods Mitch and his brothers had gone through without a cohesive parental presence in their lives, it explained a lot.

And, as Connor sometimes reminded them, Pops didn't drink *and* chase women. He merely drank.

Now the opposite was true: Pops no longer drank, he, um, chased women. Or at least one, if Mitch's suspicions were true.

Mitch tried to stretch the kinks from his neck. He really didn't need this heaped on top of everything else that had happened since last night.

"On second thought, I'm going to skip breakfast this morning," Sean said. "I think I'll go catch a quick shower instead."

"Yeah," Mitch said absently. "Why don't you do that."

Sean started to step from the room, coffee cup in hand. He halted near the door and eyed Mitch closely. Too closely. "Everything all right? Pardon the expression, but you look like you've just seen a ghost."

Mitch turned toward the counter. "The ghost of summers past, maybe," he said to himself. His intention that morning had been to unload everything and seek out some of Pops's no-nonsense, use-the-good-sense-God-gave-you advice. Now, he was afraid Pops would be talking as much about his own personal life as advising him on his. He didn't think he was up to peeking at that particular insight. "I'm fine." He cleared his throat. "By the way, this…person you stayed with last night. Anybody I know?"

Silence greeted his question. He turned back to see Pops grinning. "Uh-huh."

"Care to share who?"

"Uh-uh."

Mitch stood in the middle of the kitchen, watching in amazement as his father left the room, whistling as he went.

Mitch left the coffee on, snatched up his truck keys, then headed for the door. He needed to get out of the house. All this…whistling was making him feel lousier.

AH, THIS WAS more like it. Good, familiar company, a hot cup of coffee, and peace in which to drink it.

One of the many advantages of having traded his P.I. cap in for his new one as a horse breeder was his ability to structure his day however he liked. During the week it was easier to drop in at Bo and Ruth's Paradise Diner for breakfast and lunch before and between chores than to cook something up for himself. And on those occasions when he traveled into D.C. to work on the few cases he'd held on to or to check in with Mike and Renee, he did so in the afternoon. He glanced at the date on his watch, reminding himself that he'd planned to head into the city tomorrow.

He'd completely forgotten.

Stiffening, he told himself that he was *not* going to think of the person behind his recent distracted state.

Mitch leaned his elbows against the counter and took a deep breath of his first cup of Joe. Even on his good days he couldn't come close to imitating Ruth's unique blend. And today was definitely *not* one of his good days.

But it was getting better.

Farther down the counter he listened with half an ear as the ever-present Darton brothers argued about whose turn it was to buy breakfast, and behind him he heard Ezra, owner of the town's only gas station, order his usual pizza, despite that it was nine o'clock in the morning. But it was Sharon, the waitress's, tight little uniform that got his attention as she reached for a plate of bacon and eggs on the other side of the counter. What a great pair of legs.

She's too young for you, his conscience taunted.

She's legal, his libido argued back.

The cash register free of customers, Ruth stepped up to fill a glass of water for him. Mitch dragged his gaze from Sharon's legs and smiled his greeting.

"Didn't expect to see you in this morning," Ruth said.

"You and Sean normally eat breakfast at the house on Sundays, don't you?"

Mitch's grin waned. "Pops had, um, other things on his agenda today."

"I see."

He slowly sipped at his coffee. No doubt Ruth saw a whole lot more than the rest of them did. Born and raised in Manchester, she took great pride in letting everyone know she was never interested in living anywhere else. A good twenty years Mitch's senior, she had an uncanny ability to figure out what was going on before anyone else did—including those involved in the goings-on.

"By the way, pass on to your brother that Bo and I had a grand ol' time at the reception last night. It's been so long since anyone from these parts has gotten married, I'd forgotten what a wedding looked like."

Mitch put down his cup. "I'll tell Marc when he and Mel get back. I get the impression calling home isn't going to be at the top of their list right now." He waved at Bo through the open kitchen window. Bo raised a meaty hand in response, looking more like a bouncer than a cook. "For a couple that likes to close down the joint, you guys left a little early, didn't you?"

Ruth busied herself clearing the spot next to him. "Bo was a little tired, that's all. Things were pretty hectic around here yesterday, and what with the drive into Maryland and all…well, I guess it all caught up with him last night."

Mitch frowned as he watched Bo flip a few pancakes then drag the back of his hand across his forehead. Bo never got tired.

Ruth sighed. "Nice girl, that Mel. And pretty, too. Who'd have thought Marc would hook someone like her?"

Sharon angled her way back behind the counter to pick up

an order. Mitch watched her absently. "Yeah, who'd have thought."

"Enjoying the view?" Ruth asked as she dragged a rag across the counter in front of him.

Mitch grinned at her. "Yeah."

Sharon shot him a coy little smile as she squeezed out from behind the counter to take Ezra his breakfast pizza. Ruth put her rag away and leaned closer to him.

He told himself he didn't care what she was about to say. He lifted the cup to his lips. Nothing was going to stop him from enjoying his first cup of coffee.

Ruth said, "You'll probably enjoy the view a whole lot more tomorrow morning when Liz comes back to work."

Mitch spewed the coffee out all over the counter. What precious little peace he'd managed to find scattered to the four winds, and his frustration level surged past the danger point.

Ruth smiled, tossed him the rag to clean up the mess, then walked pleased as could be toward the kitchen.

ADMIT IT, McCoy, you're thinking with the wrong body part.

Mitch pulled his pickup over a low rise and slowed to a stop on the weed-choked gravel road. He stared at the hulking Victorian some fifty yards away. Not just any hulking Victorian, but Liz's hulking Victorian. Just knowing she was in it—alone—did interesting things to his body.

He dragged in a deep breath and let loose a line of unmatched curses. Who in the hell had decided to boot him out of his familiar life and into a twisted version of Oz?

Mitch scrubbed his hand over his face. In this particular instance, he could count the bricks that led to the unfamiliar territory in which he now wandered around stupidly. First, Liz had slunk back into town in that shiny new car. Next, Pops had rambled in, looking like he'd come fresh from licking some woman's neck, his off-tune whistling chasing Mitch straight from the house, bursting with the urge to do some of his own neck-licking. Then Ruth had spilled the beans about Liz's returning to work at the diner. Soon thereafter he found out word was already all around about her impulsive return. Everyone at the diner was abuzz with the news. Even Josiah—who did little more than rock in his chair on the general store porch—had said something about her still being the tallest drink of water this side of the Appalachians. This when the old guy had barely said anything to anyone for years.

That had been the last straw. Who else but Liz could invade every corner of his life in less than twelve hours without even trying? So he'd abandoned his plans to have breakfast then return to the house to start laying pipe from the house to the new barn, and headed out to the old Braden place.

Mitch took his foot off the brake and steered his truck over the remainder of the potholed, deeply rutted drive. Goliath barked beside him. He looked at the little traitor. How, after living in D.C. with him for several years, could the damn dog remember this ramshackle house and the fact that Liz lived here?

Correction. Had occasionally lived here. She might be visiting, but Mitch had no illusions that Liz was staying, despite her having taken on her old job. She was merely a visitor in a place she, herself, had once described as never really having been home.

He ground the truck to a halt next to a weeping willow and shut off the engine. While Old Man Peabody had managed to keep time from touching the house itself much, the surrounding greenery had been left to run wild. Trees that had been little more than saplings now towered over the truck. The lilac bush was so overgrown, it would take a chainsaw to cut it back. The grass was nearly up to the middle of his shins....

The sight of the grass sent him reeling back to a time when he was seventeen and had decided to make a good impression on Liz's grandmother by offering to mow the yard. A grand gesture that had turned into a disaster when he found out exactly how *much* grass he would have to mow. Using Minerva Braden's old push mower, it had taken him all afternoon.

Ah, but it had been worth it. He smiled. The sun had been setting, the lights inside the house just switching on, and he'd caught a glimpse of Liz—who would have been all of a tender fourteen then and well on her way to being built like Marilyn Monroe—through her bedroom window, exploring her blossoming curves in a full-length mirror. He'd watched her skim her hands lightly over her breasts, pinching her pink nipples. Then she slid her fingers down over her still-boyish hips, then back up over her inner thighs, pausing where her soft curls sprang against the white cotton of her panties....

Sweat caused by a whole different source had soaked him, his own shallow breathing sounded foreign to his ears...much as it sounded now.

Mitch closed his eyes to banish the vivid image and to ease his acute physical reaction to it. It was only natural that being near Liz again would open a door to the past. He only wished that door would reveal as much of the bad as the good.

He couldn't help wondering if he'd be in the sorry state he was if he and Liz had ever...well, if they had ever had sex. If they hadn't waited for the wedding night that had never come, and if he had had what he'd been only dreaming about.

He reached for the ignition, then dropped his hand again.

For the fifth time that morning, he told himself he'd be better off to lie low and wait for her inevitable departure to happen. But he couldn't. Not when he knew the only reason she'd have returned to Manchester would be because she had to be in some sort of trouble.

And not when his testosterone level had reached an all-time high, leaving him little more than a quivering sack of lust.

He climbed out of the truck and waited for the aging Goliath to leap down. His stout body appeared to shudder as his paws met the hard earth, then he lumbered in the direction of a stand of trees on the north side of the property. Shaking his head, Mitch shut the door and stepped around the side of the house, noting the weeds pushing through the thin gravel of the drive. Near the one-car garage some twenty feet behind the house, he spotted the Lexus. A large green tarp he suspected was a tent was draped over the roof and hood. Little was visible except for half the Massachusetts license plate.

Interesting....

He might have believed she'd covered the vehicle to protect it from the elements, if it weren't for the bloodstained wedding dress she'd been wearing when she drove the car into town. And her elusive answers to his questions.

"Hello?" he called through the screen door. He made out the tinny sound of a radio and stared through the screen at wet wading boots in the mudroom...right next to the pair of strappy red shoes she'd been wearing last night.

He called out again—no response. He grasped the tarnished handle and tugged the door open, cringing at the bone-chilling screech of the rusty hinges.

"I'm in the kitchen!"

Mitch stepped over the boots, knowing it had to be Liz who invited him in. Who else would welcome Lord only knew who into the house? He froze in the open doorway to the roomy, sun-filled kitchen.

"Oh, it's you. Tell me why I'm not surprised," she said casually. She stood in front of the sink, yards of white fabric pooled around her feet. She yanked on the material, stuffing a good portion of it under running water.

Mitch tried to come up with a finely honed comeback, but doubted the words would make it past his closed throat anyway. His gaze moved of its own leisurely accord. Up from her slender bare feet and purple-painted toe nails, over the shapely length of her long, tanned legs to where a pair of cut-off jeans barely covered her firmly rounded bottom. He shifted until his gaze rested on the jaggedly cut edge of the Georgetown University T-shirt, an indecent scrap of cotton that came dangerously close to hiking up over her breasts. Breasts he guessed were bare given the way they swayed as she shoved the white material into the sink.

Seven years ago the outfit had been tomboyish on her almost too-slender body. Now it was downright sinful given her fuller, lusher curves.

He pushed a swallow past his dry throat and stared at her golden hair.

"You're blond," he said, staring at the way the sunlight made the shoulder-length straight tresses glow. The impact of her looking so much like she had before was like a blow to the stomach.

"Life as a brunette wasn't as lucky as I thought it would be," she said, motioning toward an empty box of hair coloring on the cluttered counter. He caught her gaze. There must have been something on his face that gave him away because she bit her bottom lip and touched a hand to her head. "What's the matter? Did I miss a spot or something?" When she plopped her hand back in the sink, water splashed onto the threadbare front of the T-shirt. Mitch caught sight of the tightening of her nipples beneath the soft cotton, then forcibly wrenched his gaze away.

"No, it's fine. It's great. Couldn't you find anything else to wear?" He plucked a travel brochure from the table and held it strategically in front of himself where his jeans had grown snug. He hadn't gotten a hard-on so easily since... He cursed. Since he'd last seen Liz in the same outfit.

He stared at the other items on the table. More brochures, maps and travel guides littered the top, some dog-eared, others apparently untouched. He frowned and slid a map of Dallas aside, finding another pamphlet on Miami underneath.

"I don't know if you noticed, but I didn't exactly have a suitcase with me when I rolled into town." Liz drew his attention back to her. She turned off the water and rubbed the shining wet material together.

Oh, no you don't, he warned himself, as his gaze yearned to watch how her breasts responded to the vigorous movement of her arms.

"It was the only thing in the house I could find that still fit," she said between determined attacks on the dress.

Fit. She was certainly stretching the definition of that word. Then again, his own jeans had fit just fine until he came into the house.

Agitated, he rustled the brochure he held and focused his gaze on her slender hands. It suddenly struck him what she was doing.

She's washing the bloodstain from the wedding dress.

Or at least she was trying to. Judging from the puddles of water on the countertop and around her bare feet—were her toenails really painted fluorescent purple?—she had been trying for some time with little luck.

If anything could have cooled him down, her intentions

did. He put the brochure back onto the table. "What are you doing, Liz?"

She shrugged off his question as she wiped her damp forehead on her shirtsleeve. "Thought I'd do a little laundry this morning."

He was frustrated, not only by her evasion of his question, but by the way his libido was so acutely focused on her tight little behind and the delectable curves of her flesh. He stuffed his hands into his jeans pockets, wincing as the coarse denim pulled tighter across certain strategic areas.

"Uh-huh."

She looked at him then, her hazel eyes filled with amusement while her hands kept up their rapid motion. "You wouldn't happen to know how to get rid of bloodstains, would you?"

Mitch pinched the bridge of his nose. "Try sponging on some peroxide."

Her luscious mouth curved into a smile.

"I was raised with four brothers, remember?"

She turned back to the sink, giving him full rein to do what he would with the view. "How could I forget? Your brothers hardly left us alone for a minute."

"That's because they were all in lust with you." *And so was I.*

Her throaty laugh made him want to groan. "I can't imagine Jake being in lust with anyone."

"Yeah, well, you never saw the shrine he built for you in his room." Mitch quickly reached his patience level, which was odd, because he hadn't known he had one. He stepped forward and grabbed her arms, forcing her to face him.

"Liz, what in the hell are you doing back here? And just what...what in the hell is going on?"

The surprised shadow on her face made him want to groan all over again. Now that she had returned to her natural hair color, the electric shade of her eyes was enhanced, making it nearly impossible to look anywhere else.

Nothing about this woman was constant, smooth. Not her personality, not her actions, and certainly not her physical traits. Her nose sloped, her chin was an angular work of art with a tiny little dimple in the middle. But it was her too-wide, lavish mouth that had always done him in.

"Mitch?" she practically purred, and, if anyone could purr, Liz certainly could.

"Hmmm?" he hummed distractedly, falling into the hazel depths of her eyes.

"I hope you realize you're going to be the one to mop up the mess you're making."

Mess? He hadn't made a mess yet, but give him a couple more seconds, and—

He blinked, watching as her hands dripped water on the floor.

"I just spent the morning mopping up the basement after a pipe burst. I don't much want to clean up the kitchen floor, too."

He released her so fast, she nearly toppled to the floor. He remembered the wet hip boots in the mudroom.

"I hope you turned off the electricity before you went trudging through that water," he grumbled, trying to get a handle on himself. He was supposed to be trying to convince her to get into her car and head for the road, not entertaining thoughts of getting her between the sheets.

"What electricity? Old Man Peabody kept the water on, but it's going to take some money to get the electricity switched back on."

Mitch glanced at a one-eyed propane burner on top of the obsolete stove, and a lantern near a cot in the corner. "So that's why you took your old job back at the diner."

She tilted her head and slid her gaze over him suggestively. "Are you going to tell me what you're doing here, or am I going to have to guess?" She tugged on the bottom of her T-shirt, pulling it tight against her breasts in a provocative way, though she was likely preventing the scrap of material from revealing more than was decent. "Or did you just come out to hassle me?"

"It depends on your definition of hassle," he said, not trusting the spark of mischief that compelled him to grin. "If you categorize wanting to know what you're doing as hassling you, then we have a problem."

"The only problem I'm having now is getting the stain out of that dress."

Mitch stared at the sopping wet material puddled on the chipped tile floor. "That's just it. Why would you want to get the stain out?" He eyed her. "Unless, of course, you intend to use the dress again."

He didn't miss her amused expression. She turned from him and hoisted the dress up onto the counter.

He stepped closer until he was nearly flush with her backside. The subtle scent of wild cherries drifted over him, inciting another uncomfortable response in the lower half of his body.

"Tell me, Liz, why is it there's a car parked out back that costs more than some houses and you can't afford to have your electricity turned on?"

His breath stirred her honey-blond hair. He felt satisfied at her soft sigh.

He reached around her and touched the satiny material of the wedding dress, purposely skimming his arm against hers. "And why are you trying so hard to wash that stain out?"

She turned in his arms, staring up at him as if she just now realized how close he was. The tips of her breasts grazed his chest and this time *he* sighed—or choked, more accurately. A reaction she didn't miss if the teasing smile on her lips was anything to go by.

"What's the matter, Mitch? Are you thinking that this time I didn't just run out on my groom? That maybe this time I did away with him?"

He narrowed his eyes. Despite the way she trembled, she was acting too casual, too self-composed. "Well, that would certainly answer a lot of questions." He caught a lock of her blond hair and twirled the silky strands around his finger. "The first being why you came back to Manchester."

A SHIVER swept down Liz's neck despite the late June sunshine that drenched the kitchen through the window above the sink. The combination of hot sunshine on her back and one hundred percent Mitch McCoy at her front was a lethal one. She pressed her rear against the sharp edge of the counter.

"I already told you why I came back."

"No, Liz," Mitch shook his head. "You didn't tell me why. You said what it would take for you to leave. More specifically, that things had to settle down in Boston before you could move on." His gaze shifted to her mouth and she had to fight not to lick her suddenly dry lips. "What I want to know is what things need to settle down and why."

Liz felt incredibly, wickedly, exposed standing like that in front of him. Hardly a thing in her old bedroom upstairs fit. And despite her affected nonchalance when he'd commented on her apparel, the first thing she'd wanted to do when she'd spotted him in the doorway was cover herself from his searing gaze. The problem was the only other things that fit were her wedding dress and—thankfully—her old waitressing uniform.

She rode out a shiver that began at the tips of her toes and flitted all the way up to her scalp. Who would have thought that after seven years Mitch would still make her want to strip naked and run through the cornfields with him?

"Don't worry, Mitch. I'm no longer the damsel in distress you once had to rescue at every turn. I'm perfectly capable of taking care of myself now."

His green eyes darkened. "This isn't a matter of stealing a candy bar from Obernauer's, Liz. Or your filling Peabody's firing-range cans with cement. Answer my question."

Her smile was decidedly playful. "Is that why you came all the way out here? Because you think I'm in some sort of trouble?"

His expression grew teasing as his gaze raked her humming body. "I'm just trying to protect the residents of Manchester, Liz."

"From little ol' me?"

"Yes, from you. From you and whoever is following on your heels."

Following on my heels. So he hadn't forgotten what she'd said on the dark road last night. Her smile widened.

"Don't worry. I'd never put anybody in Manchester in danger."

"Why don't you let me be the judge of that? For once, why don't you tell me exactly what's going on?"

She wriggled to free herself without touching him. An impossible task with him so near. She shifted to her right and he compensated for the move, leaning in closer. Her highly sensitive nipples brushed against the hard width of his chest a second time and she gasped, arousal heating her insides and a thrill of awareness tingling across every inch of her skin, exposed or otherwise. His hands caressed her arms and she shivered.

"I...I wouldn't do that if I were you," she whispered, overly interested in the nearness of his mouth.

"Do what?"

"Kiss me."

A maddening grin played on his all-too-tempting lips. "Then stop me."

He made the inches separating them disappear, pressing the solid muscles of his thighs against her legs, the scrape of rough denim against her tender skin excitingly erotic. His mouth stopped a hairbreadth away from hers, his minty breath fanning her heated cheeks, his eyes inviting her to finish what he had begun. She swallowed hard, incapable of stopping him...incapable of stopping herself. She groaned.

Oh, how she'd missed the feel of him against her.

Thrusting her fingers into his thick brown hair, she drew him the rest of the way, crushing his lips against hers, challenging him to a duel of tongues, an exchange of pleasure she'd never felt as powerfully with anyone else. He responded with consummate flair, pulling her bottom lip into his mouth and gently biting down on it, then claiming her in a way she remembered all too well. Liz's entire body caught fire. She restlessly, instinctively sought closer contact. A low whimper caught in her throat as the ridge of his arousal pressed provocatively against the cradle of her thighs.

Her hands were suddenly all over him. In his hair, tugging his T-shirt from his jeans, sculpting his firm backside. She couldn't seem to touch him nearly enough. From rough denim to velvety hot skin to the thick strands of his hair, her hands sought something she couldn't hope to define...not until his fingers found the skin over her rib cage.

She caught her breath, her mouth stilling beneath his, her eyes locking with his half-lidded ones. *Touch me,* she silently pleaded. Her nipples strained painfully against the thin cotton of her shirt. Her chest rose and fell as she regained her breath and dragged in precious air. Irrationally, she thought she'd die if he didn't touch her.

His fingers slid up, gently cupping the underside of her

breasts. Heat, sure and swift, swept over her in dizzying waves. Liz nearly collapsed to the floor in a puddle of shimmering need. One callused thumb moved over her right nipple. She moaned.

"Ohh," she whispered, tugging her mouth from his, trying to catch her breath, calm the thick pulsing of her heart.

Mitch suddenly jerked back, taking his warmth with him. Liz propped her hands against her knees, filled with the sudden urge to laugh.

The picture really was quite ludicrous. Yesterday she had been about to marry another man. Now she was practically devouring Mitch.

This didn't make any sense at all.

"Why don't we continue this conversation another time?" she asked, dragging the back of her knuckles across her swollen lips. "I have a lot of things I need to do today, and your kissing me isn't going to help get them done."

His grin was decidedly devilish, despite the questioning glint in his eyes. "I didn't kiss you, Liz. You kissed me. Remember?"

Oh, yeah, she remembered all right. And if he didn't leave *now*, she was going to pin him to the table.

"Answer my question and I'll be happy to let you get on with your list of chores."

Liz straightened. "Well, then, I think you oughta just strip and let's get on with it."

He stumbled backward as if she had physically pushed him. The edge of the table stopped his progress. "What?"

"That's the real reason you came here, isn't it, Mitch?" There was something wonderfully delicious about the expression on his face. "You came to get what you couldn't have seven years ago."

3

YOU CAME to get what you couldn't have seven years ago.

Mitch clenched his coffee cup, mulling over what Liz had said the day before. He shifted uncomfortably on the diner stool. He cursed, remembering how he'd beat a hasty retreat out of her house like a panicked roadrunner.

It was past noon on Monday. The diner was packed. His coffee was getting cold. And he should be on the road to D.C., where he'd planned to catch up on some office work and check in with a couple of clients...as well as do some more checking on the ghost of weddings past and present. Instead, he was in the diner, gaping at the broken pieces of his sorry life, and staring at the bomb in a waitress uniform that had broken it.

Leaving Liz's house yesterday after relearning the taste of her mouth, feeling her hot, slick flesh against his, had been one of the hardest things he'd ever done. How much he'd have liked to have slid his fingers up under the frayed hem of her jean shorts and explored the hot, pliant flesh there. How much he had yearned to claim—as she had so slyly suggested—what had been denied him so many years ago.

But the instant she'd offered up what had once been forbidden fruit, he'd hightailed it out of there.

He'd spent the bulk of this morning alternately taking cold showers—it was a hot day, damn it—and checking with the Virginia and Massachusetts state law officials. Several calls yielded no outstanding warrants. There was absolutely nothing on her listed at the FBI's National Crime Information Center, including info on whether or not the Lexus was stolen. Not stopping there, he contacted the Massachusetts Department of Motor Vehicles; the plates on the Lexus were hers, as was the Lexus itself, though he found it interesting that the Boston address in the DMV's files was no longer valid.

What bothered him was that he couldn't verify one way or another whether or not she had skipped town *before* or *after* her wedding ceremony. An irritating clerk he had talked to at the licensing bureau refused to tell him anything that wasn't already a part of public record and said she wasn't his gofer. If he wanted the information, he'd have to go fish it out himself...when it was publicly posted in a week or two.

At least his next call had gone better. He'd found Liz listed as owner of Braden Consulting in the State Board of Corporations' books.

He stared at the address and phone number to that business now and sucked in a deep breath, puffing his cheeks out as he released it.

He stuffed the number back into his pocket, telling himself he should be more concerned with all the work that had gone undone around the McCoy place, and just when, exactly, he planned to head out for D.C. He'd wished Pops had been around, but the old man had been gone when he returned from Liz's yesterday, and Mitch had the sneaking suspicion he hadn't made it home again last night.

Mitch sipped his cold coffee, masking the uneasiness twisting inside him like a twenty-foot length of knotted razor wire.

Down the counter from him, he tuned in Moses Darton complaining about the puny size of his Heavenly Pineapple Ribs for the third time and asking Liz if she couldn't scare up a bigger slab. She sighed in exasperation and slid the refused plate onto the counter to go back into the kitchen.

"Your halo's slipping, angel," he said to her in a voice almost too low to make out in the packed diner. Hell, figuratively speaking, her halo had fallen off a long time ago.

"After yesterday, I think you passed on the chance to call me angel, Mitch." She tugged on the hem of her white skirt to hide the thighs he'd already taken an eyeful of.

"Hmm." He tilted his head, taking in his fill. He openly followed the line down the front of her uniform, then stared at her legs. "Maybe."

He watched that simmering, wicked smile light her eyes before she tugged up the edge of the *Manchester Journal* he held.

"Read your paper, McCoy. I wouldn't want you to miss an important news flash."

"Funny, I was just checking for any possible news on you."

He peered over the paper to find her running that pink tongue of hers over her lips. His gut-deep reaction almost made him groan.

What was it about this one woman? Just when he thought he had finally shaken off the baggage he'd been hauling around since she'd left and was eager to re-start his life, she popped back in and piled the overpacked trunks back up on his shoulders again. Reminded him that he had never completely cleansed her from his system.

Perhaps it was time he did.

The thought snagged in his mind and held.

He grinned. He'd been uncomfortable ever since scurrying from her grandmother's house yesterday. Now he knew why. He should have stayed. Should have peeled those skimpy shorts down her long, long legs and taken what she'd offered. Maybe if he had, he wouldn't be sitting there wondering what would have happened if he had. Maybe he wouldn't be sitting there wanting her more with every breath he took.

He grimaced. And maybe he'd be even worse off.

During training at Quantico, he'd learned to look at problems from all angles, and that particular angle bothered him. Having sex with Liz Braden might very well be just what he needed to rid her from his life forever. It might also be the catalyst to finding himself in the same damn boat he'd been in seven years ago.

He lifted the paper this time, hiding himself from her curious gaze.

What other alternative did he have but to finish what had been started so long ago?

And just consider the fringe benefits....

He rustled his paper. "Angel? You mind giving me a warm-up over here?"

WARM-UP?

Liz glanced at Mitch McCoy. She didn't miss the suggestion threaded through his innocuous words, or the all-too-familiar emotions that emerged whenever she looked his way.

Taking the coffeepot from the warmer, she poured some of the hot liquid into his almost-full cup. It was all too...weird being here again, in the same role she'd played so long ago, as soon as she was old enough to apply for the waitressing job. In a town the size of Manchester, where "downtown" consisted of little more than a city block, the only choice she'd had job-wise was at the diner, since the general store was well-manned by Charles Obernauer and his wife, Hannah.

Then there was Mitch....

It wasn't what Mitch said that got to her. It was the way he said it. Whenever he talked to her, a wicked proposition hummed through his words, sending tiny little shivers scooting everywhere.

Mitch took a long sip, then grinned. "Oh, and I could do with a piece of Paradise Pie, too."

"Oh, you could, could you?"

"Uh-huh."

She removed the apple pie from the counter display and turned out a healthy piece, smothering it with vanilla ice cream and sticking a candy cherub on top. She pushed the plate in front of him as his gaze slid over her tight white uniform and lingered on the hem. Tiny tingles followed his path and Liz drew in an uneven breath.

"Am I getting under your skin, Liz?" he asked. "You used to like it when I teased you."

Her gaze flicked from his eyes to his mouth as he took a hefty bite of pie, then quickly to his eyes again. She quietly cleared her throat, finding him far more appealing than was safe. A little closer and she'd give him a repeat performance of what had passed between them yesterday.

Yes, he was getting under her skin, by making her want to feel him all over it.

He lifted his eyes to hers, that damnable teasing glint giving him a wholly devilish appearance. "Are you going to answer me?"

"Answer you?" She cleared her throat, trying to recall the question. Oh, yes, her skin and his getting under it. "It's been a long time since...then." So long she had a hard time recognizing the woman who once thought she could make a man like Mitch happy.

Her gaze riveted to a dab of vanilla ice cream at the side of his mouth. She longed to be able to lean over and lap it off.

"And the next thing would be?" he prompted.

"Next thing?"

He nodded and swallowed another bite.

I want to know why you never came after me, her heart answered.

Her breath caught and she raised her gaze to his eyes. Flames seemed to backlight the green depths as he apparently tried to gauge what she was thinking.

"Don't you dare look at me that way," she said.

"Look at you what way?"

Her voice was little more than a throaty rasp. "You know what way. That look that, um, says you'd rather be watching me melt instead of the ice cream in front of you."

The right side of his well-defined mouth budged up a fraction of an inch as he licked off the ice cream. "It is what I'd rather be doing, so why shouldn't my expression say that?"

Liz smoothed the collar of her uniform. "Because I don't want to be your ice cream, that's why." *Liar.* She eyed his left hand slowly inching across the counter. His fingertips lightly grazed her arm in a maddening path he followed back and forth.

"What...what are you doing?"

"I'm thinking."

She moved his hand back across the counter and planted it in his half-eaten pie. "Since when does it take fingers to think?"

"Since your explanation of why you don't like my attention has nothing to do with your lack of attraction to me." He watched her while he cleaned the ice cream from his hand with a napkin, then he dipped his fingers in his water glass and shook them once in her direction.

She wiped the droplets of water from her cheek, surprised they hadn't sizzled against the heat of her skin. "Lack of attraction? Are you trying to say what I think you are?"

"What?" He picked up his fork and stabbed another piece

of pie. "That you're wildly attracted to me and don't know what to do about it?"

"Wildly attracted?"

"Uh-huh." His eyes challenged her.

"I, um, at one time I might have been very attracted to you, Mitch McCoy—" her voice softened "—but now I wouldn't even consider..."

"Sleeping with me?"

Her muscles liquefied, but somehow she managed to push out, "You already missed your opportunity there. From here on out, something like that will only happen in your dreams."

He nodded. "Yep, there, too." He finished the last of his pie and shook his head. "Only I know for sure I'm not dreaming now. Because if I were, you wouldn't be on the other side of the counter, and you wouldn't be wearing that uniform, no matter how cute you look in it."

"Oh? And where, um, would I be?"

His pupils widened, threatening to take over the green of his eyes. "For starters, you'd be stretched across this counter with those long legs of yours..."

Liz quickly took a step back, her pulse leaping. "That's enough. I think I get the picture."

"But darlin', you didn't even let me get to the part about what *I* was doing."

A bolt of awareness sliced through Liz's abdomen. No, he hadn't told her what he'd been doing in his dream, but she could very well imagine. And the images were more than distracting, they were downright provocative—especially when combined with the confusing heat that still lingered from the day before. She cleared her throat and turned away. She'd never look at the long, narrow slip of counter the same way again.

"Look," Ezra called out from a corner booth. "Lizzie is quiet. Looks like Mitch has struck a chord."

"I don't have any chords to strike," Liz lied. "I was just thinking that Mitch's vivid imagination is exactly why everyone calls him a dreamer." Still, she tried to ignore the sensation similar to a quivering harp string twanging straight through her.

"Hey, Mitch," Ezra said, "are we all included in your little...dream?"

Liz stared at him as he slowly shook his head. "Nope. Sorry, Ez, it's just me and Lizzie in this scenario. That's what makes it a dream."

His gaze said a whole hell of a lot more than his words. Was he threatening her? Was he saying in a cryptic way that the next time they were alone she might not get off so easy?

This flirtatious attitude was the last thing she'd expected from him. Where were the questions? Evidence of the huge ding to his pride? After all, seven years ago she had left him standing at the altar. She wiped the counter, then stuffed the rag back into her apron pocket. He showed neither. Instead, he slanted her a few unexpected zingers that short-circuited her own emotional wiring, leaving her inexplicably responsive to his teasing.

He finished his pie then picked up the paper folded at his elbow, his grin telling her he knew he'd hit his mark.

She looked around the diner and found nothing out of the ordinary. Which was laughable because anyone else might find *everything* out of the ordinary. From the padded pink vinyl booths, the corny cherubs on the tabletops that swayed back and forth when the customers moved, to the townsfolk who were as peculiar as the decor, Liz had forgotten how...eccentric the town was. How familiar and reassuringly unchanged. All too easily she recalled how Gran brought her here for lunch every Sunday after church service. How the McCoy bunch had teased her when she was fourteen and had finally grown breasts. How she had screwed up every order on her first day at work, and how everyone had covertly played musical plates when they thought she wasn't looking and had generously tipped her anyway.

She turned the pages of her order pad and tallied up the total for table one.

She was just being sentimental. Yes, that's what it was. That's the reason she'd succumbed to the desire to kiss Mitch in Gran's kitchen, why his nearness and flirting had such a hot effect on her now. Certainly nothing that would get in the way of her plans to move on with her life, go somewhere where she could set up her business all over again. Plans that had nothing to do with Mitch or Manchester or the nineteen hundred and ninety-nine residents that inhabited the north-central Virginia town, no matter how reassuringly familiar they all were. Plans she fully intended to see succeed before her thirtieth birthday less than two weeks from now.

Thirty years old. She nearly groaned and wondered if she should order her headstone now.

Mid-tally, Liz halted her pencil and flipped to another page in her order book. Tearing it off, she slid the white slip under the wall of the *Manchester Journal.*

Mitch dropped the newspaper a few inches, gazing at her with those teasing green eyes of his.

"Not in a hurry to get rid of me, are you, angel?"

"Now, Mitch, why would you say that?" She leaned her hips against the counter and offered up a smile. "How many times do I have to ask before you stop calling me angel?"

He shook his paper as if to straighten it, though his gaze remained riveted to her face. "Ask as often as you like. I'm not going to stop. Not as long as you're in front of me wearing that white uniform." The grin that threatened grew into blood-heating reality.

Every inch of her roused to glorious life. "Is that your way of saying you want *me* to leave?"

"That's not my way of saying anything except what I said." He rustled the paper again.

She twisted her lips and allowed her gaze to flick slowly over his face. *This is his way of getting back at me*, she realized. No angry demands to know why she'd left. No attempts to get her alone for a quiet talk. Not even any mention of the time they'd been together or the scorching kiss they'd shared yesterday. No, Mitch McCoy intended to make her time here as miserable as possible. And if he could speed up the process of her leaving, it was all for the better.

The maddening thing of it was that, despite everything, she wanted to have him hosed down and brought to her tent...*pronto*.

"Isn't there someplace you should be getting back to? Doesn't the world need saving or something?" she said, reaching for his paper again. He moved the *Journal* out of reach.

"I didn't know you paid that close attention to my comings and goings."

She crossed her arms over her chest. "The diner's pretty full. We could use the spot you're taking for someone interested in eating." She smiled. "Anyway, I'm more interested in your goings than your comings, Mitch."

"Funny, I'd say you're more interested in *your* goings than your comings." He stretched lazily, offering every solid part of his T-shirt-covered abdomen for inspection. Liz covertly admired the enticing wall of muscle, then turned away, a slow burn beginning in the pit of her stomach. She was wrong. More had changed about him than his unpredictability. No longer was he the corded teenager, then young man for whom she had once hungered. A few pounds of added muscle made his physique more intriguing, more enticing, and much more irresistible than it had ever been.

She pushed open the kitchen door, aware of his keen attention.

"Hey, Bo, how are the burgers frying?" She flashed a smile at the harried cook and half-owner of the diner.

"They're...frying," he said gruffly.

"Mind if I use the phone for a minute?"

"Naw." He waved toward the extension on the wall near the door. "Go on ahead."

"Thanks."

She plucked the receiver from the old rotary phone, dialed the area code for Boston, then the number to her office. She'd called her personal assistant, Sheila, from the general store yesterday. She only hoped she'd like the answers she was going to get today.

"Hello?"

Liz wound the tangled cord around her finger. "Not even Braden Consulting anymore, huh?"

Sheila sighed heavily into the receiver. "Nope. My boss told me the business is defunct as of yesterday." Despite her words, Liz imaged the young woman smiling. She'd promised her a severance that would equal six months pay, enough for Sheila to follow her dream of opening her own dance school. "Hi, Liz. Funny you should call this second. I just hung up with your mother."

"Sunny?" Liz repeated, surprised. Why would her mother be calling her?

"Yeah. She seemed rushed and didn't talk long, but said she's been trying to contact you since the day of the wedding that never was."

She cringed at the description. "What did you tell her?"

Sheila hesitated. "In all honesty, I wasn't sure what to tell her. So I told her nothing."

That meant her assistant had stuck to the story she'd given her, which was to basically claim she hadn't talked to her and didn't know where she was. Liz bit her bottom lip. "Did she leave a number I can call?"

"No. She said she's unreachable now, but that she'd try back."

Good ol' consistent Mom. She was likely in between moves and didn't have a phone. The cell phone Liz had given her for Christmas had been lost, never to be found again. She suspected Sunny had tossed it out the same day she got it. Too restrictive, is how she'd viewed the modern piece of technology.

"So, what do you have for me?"

Sheila paused, then said, "You want the bad news, the bad news...or the bad news?"

"Why don't we start with the bad news?"

She heard the closing of a filing cabinet and guessed Sheila was already closing up shop. "You were right. Beschloss froze all your accounts, business and personal. And he filed assault charges against you. The cops were by this morning."

Liz rubbed her forehead. "And the bad news?"

"You broke his nose." There was a short burst of laughter. "He's got this...contraption on his face that makes him look like an alien from *The Next Generation*."

Liz groaned.

"Serves him right, really. I always thought he was a reptile."

"I only wish I had listened to you."

Another whoosh of a cabinet drawer. "Hmm...I seem to recall you couldn't hear me over the ticking of that biological clock of yours. Something about turning thirty—"

"Call me in six years and tell me how you feel then, smartie pants." She really was going to miss Sheila. She'd been like a little sister to her for the year she was in Boston.

"Liz? You want me to call those cops back and report Beschloss? I could probably have access to your accounts by this time tomorrow. And it might get that charge of assault dropped." She paused. "Either that, or you could come back and straighten everything out yourself."

"Can't do that," Liz said quietly. That was Rule One in Liz's Moving On Handbook. She never returned to a place she'd left behind. Well, except for Manchester, but that didn't count because she had a house here. In fact, yesterday she'd made arrangements to have Sheila pack up her stuff and put it all into storage, including her personal belongings when Rich finally came to his senses. Then once she was settled, Sheila was to forward it all to her new address.

Besides, going back to Boston meant speaking to her ex-fiancé, something she really didn't want to do right now—especially since it wouldn't change anything, and it might very well find her spending a little time in a jail cell.

No, she would wait this one out.

She sucked in her bottom lip, then sighed. "No. He's bound to cool down in a few days, which will take care of both problems." As much as the prospect of having Richard arrested appealed to her, he'd suffered enough. It couldn't have been easy for him to have to explain the situation to his snooty parents and the who's who of Boston society.

She spotted Mitch watching her through the open window that looked out over the dining area and waggled her fingers at him. "You go ahead and take what's in the petty cash drawer and we'll work everything out later, when things are back to normal, okay? Look, I've got to get back to...I've got to go."

"Wait. You didn't let me get to the last piece of bad news," Sheila reminded her.

Liz sighed. "You mean there's more?"

"Yeah. This guy called up this morning asking all sorts of questions about you and the business. I told him, sorry, I couldn't tell him anything because I didn't know a Liz Braden, and that we were closed for business, but he kept on. In fact, he got pretty agitated with me after asking the same questions twice."

Liz perked up. "Did he give you his name?"

"Yeah. Yeah, he did. Hold on a sec...."

Liz gazed back at the man sitting at the counter.

"Here it is. It's Mitch. Mitch McCoy."

She laughed so loud even Bo looked up from the grill. She cleared her throat and turned toward the wall. "I see."

"I take it you know this guy?" Sheila asked.

"You, um, could say that." She scratched at the body of the phone with her thumbnail. "Did he leave a number where he could be reached?"

"Yes, he did. Asked that I call him if I decided I wanted to spill."

She smiled. Sounded just like Mitch.

A few moments later, Liz hung up the receiver, then straightened the skirt of her uniform.

"Everything all right, Lizzie?" Bo asked.

"Hmm?" She looked at the man who could mirror Mel of the sitcom *Alice* right down to the white cap rolled up on his balding head. He stood behind her now. She turned to smile at him. "Shh, the guy on the other side of the window might hear you. The last thing I need now is the FBI breathing down my neck."

Bo chuckled. "Who? Mitch? Hell, Lizzie, he quit the bureau going on something like three years ago now. I thought you knew."

She mentally chewed on the tidbit. "No...I didn't."

"Not that it matters any, mind you. He started his own P.I. company along with a couple of partners in D.C."

"P.I.?" Liz scanned the features that had aged more than the years she'd been away. "What's he doing in Manchester then? Vacation?"

Bo shrugged. "Can't say as I know. Awful long time for a vacation. He came back home about eight months ago, hangs out here a bit, but doesn't talk a whole lot except for the usual conversational stuff. His brother Marc got married, did you know?"

"Yeah. I heard. Shocking, huh?" she said absently.

"Yeah. All of us around here figured out of that McCoy bunch, Mitch was the most likely to marry first."

And we both know what happened there, she added silently.

Bo headed back to the grill and she for the door. The instant it closed behind her, her gaze slammed into Mitch's.

Mitch? A P.I.?

This bit of news managed to dampen her amusement at finding out he'd been checking up on her. He'd been a tried-and-true FBI agent when she'd left. Even the one time she'd attempted to broach the subject of a career change, he'd stiffened and rattled off the reasons why his job was important to him. "Every McCoy for the last four generations has been in law enforcement, Liz. I won't be the one to break that tradition."

Now, she stared at him curiously. Something had to have happened to make him break free from that familial obligation. He was back in Manchester, wearing faded denim jeans and T-shirts that clung too perfectly to his body, reminding her of the teen he'd been before he'd taken on the responsibility that came with being born into a family where men were men and woman were... Well, where woman were non-existent.

"Tell me, Liz," he broke into her thoughts. "Did a ring

come with that wedding dress you were wearing the other night?"

"Ring?" she repeated, pretending not to know what he was referring to. She ripped off the tally for table one. "Why don't you tell me?" She smiled at the narrowing of his eyes.

"Call me old-fashioned, but usually when someone's wearing a wedding dress, it means they just got married," he baited. "Then again, I'm beginning to think a wedding dress is everyday apparel for you."

"Oh, low blow, McCoy." Liz picked up the plate Bo slid onto the window ledge. She rounded the corner, ignoring the way her skin warmed beneath Mitch's gaze.

"Here you go, Ezra, your Garden of Eden Pizza with lots of snakes, just the way you like it," she said, plopping down the anchovy- and cherry-tomato-covered pie onto table five.

"Thanks, Lizzie. I've got just enough time to give in to temptation before I've got to get back to the gas station," he said, wiping his hands on his purple and gold cotton shirt with *Ezra* sewn above the pocket. Liz piled up the empty plates left by his tablemates.

"By the way, you never did answer the question I asked earlier," Ezra said, stuffing an anchovy halfway into his mouth then sucking the rest of it in.

"What question is that?" Liz hoisted up the empty plates. "Wait, don't tell me. You're talking about that ridiculous bet again, right?"

Myra overheard her from the next table and leaned toward Liz as she passed. "You only think it's ridiculous because you're afraid of losing."

Liz eyed the wiry-haired waitress, half expecting to spot antennae hidden in the dark mass to explain the way her old friend heard everything said.

"Sorry, Ez, but I'm not much of a gambling woman."

Ezra grinned at her. "Hell, Lizzie, you used to be the first one to put your money down."

She started, realizing he was right. Then again, she used to be a lot of things she wasn't anymore. "Sorry, maybe next go-'round."

She followed Myra back behind the counter, trying to forget that Mitch sat a mere ten feet away—which was just about as easy as forgetting water was wet.

"I don't even know what this bet is about. How can I lose something I'm not even involved in?" she asked her long-ago summertime friend, pushing the dirty dishes onto the window ledge.

"You're about the only one who isn't involved." Myra's brown eyes sparkled as she plucked a leftover French fry from a plate. "Practically the whole population of Manchester has money riding on it."

Liz confiscated the fry from Myra's hand before she could eat the secondhand food. "I don't know why anyone would be interested in me."

Myra laughed and reached around her to pick at another plate. Bo pulled it into the kitchen. "Girl, your roots are buried in this town just the same as mine, even if you only nourished them during the summer. Of course everyone's interested in and concerned about you. They're also interested in the cat-and-mouse game you and Mitch have been playing since he came in this morning."

"Trust me, nothing is going on between me and Mitch."

"Come on, Liz, you can't pull the wool over this one's eyes. Anyway, it's never taken much for Ezra to start a betting pool. This particular one has to do with whether you two are going to repeat history."

Repeat history? She went still, feeling as if every drop of blood had drained from her head. In her mind's eye, she vividly remembered their wedding day....

"Oh, no," Myra said quickly. "Not *that* history. Lord forbid you should do that again. People are still talking about that."

"What history, then?"

"Well, it has something to do with the night you two were caught in here, you know, after hours, the lights on for all to see—"

Liz smiled, the sensual memory one that still haunted her dreams. "I get the picture, Myra. And I don't believe for a second that's what this bet is about."

Myra chuckled wickedly. "You're right. The only thing they're betting on is how long before you and Mitch hook up each other again."

Liz's stomach gave a funny little lilt. "Yeah? What do the odds say?"

Bo slid an order onto the counter and Myra dropped her voice an octave. "That Mitch doesn't stand a chance in hell of staying single."

Myra's laugh followed her as she collected the meals from the window and squeezed out from behind the counter to deliver them.

Liz's attention slid back to the other victim involved in the bet. She wondered just who, exactly, was supposed to be the cat and who the mouse.

She grabbed the water carafe and stepped down to refill Mitch's glass.

"Hey, Lizzie," Ezra called out. "Thought you'd like to know I got another five dollars down on the bet."

Liz looked at Mitch. "Are you responsible for this?"

"Responsible for what?"

"This bet Ezra's got going."

Mitch grinned. She felt like slugging him.

She put the water pitcher back where it belonged and rubbed her rag against the counter. "Okay, McCoy, let's get this over with right now. Ask me out, I'll tell you no and we can go on from here as if this silly bet never happened."

His grin widened. "Nope." He slowly shook his head, the overhead lights catching the golden strands otherwise lost in his thick mane of chestnut-brown hair. "I don't go out of my way to invite rejection. Not anymore."

What an odd thing to say—

"How 'bout it, angel?" he asked in that voice that rubbed her in all the right...no, *wrong* ways. "You ready to put your money where your mouth is?"

Liz dug in her pockets for her morning's tips. "How much you got down?"

"Uh-uh."

"Fine. Don't tell me then." She crumpled what she knew was no more than ten or so dollars' worth of tips. She crossed the room and put the pile of crumpled bills on the table in front of Ezra. "I don't need to know anything more than I already know. Nothing is going to happen between Mitch and me."

"Lizzie, rules are nothing over five dollars," the mechanic said quietly.

She smiled. "Is that what you're really worried about, Ez? Or are you afraid of losing your own money now that I've joined in?"

"I'll cover it."

Liz didn't turn. Didn't need to. She'd recognize the voice and the teasing tone anywhere. Mitch moved to stand behind her, carefully placing the matching funds on the table before her.

"You know, Mitch, you're really starting to ruffle my feathers," she said.

"That's my whole intention, angel."

She turned around to face him. She was unprepared to find him so...near. Before she could react, he captured a stray lock of her hair and twirled it around his thick finger, the near-white strands contrasting against his tanned, callused skin. The cocky, confident way he stood pulled his jeans tight against his muscular thighs. Her eyes followed the denim down to where his brown cowboy boots were dusty and scuffed. She swallowed.

"You don't stand a chance in hell, Mitch," she told him, mimicking Myra's words.

He tucked her hair behind her ear. "Good, 'cause that's not the place I'm counting on to help me out on this one."

THE DINER mostly emptied out after lunch. Midway through bussing table one, Liz slid into the glossy pink booth near the window, her back to Mitch, the man she feared would make her time there a study in tolerance. Oh, sure, he might have turned tail and run yesterday, but she had the sneaking suspicion he wouldn't be running anywhere else anytime soon. And after her experience with her last relationship, another man in her life was very low on her list. Especially Mitch. She'd screwed up with him before. She wasn't about to do it again. No matter how deliciously provocative his counter fantasy. Just thinking about being stretched across that counter at his complete and utter mercy made her hot all over.

She stared at the red candied cherub swaying back and forth on the table, then snatched the cheerful object from its metal spring. What had she been thinking?

"Things haven't settled down in Boston yet, huh?" Myra glided onto the seat across from her, having exchanged her uniform for a black cotton shirt and bedraggled jeans. Liz watched her tug the shirt down slightly over one smooth shoulder, her black bra strap plainly visible.

"No. In fact, they're a little worse than I expected they'd be right now." Liz accidentally snapped off one of the cherub's wings.

Mitch's rich chuckle filled the diner. Liz guessed he was still talking to Charles Obernauer, the owner of the general store. She rubbed the back of her neck to ease the tingle there.

"I know you don't know what's going on, Myra, but I do appreciate you not pushing the issue." She strained to hear the words of Mitch's conversation, then broke off the cherub's head. She tossed it onto a plate. "You were always a good friend."

"So were you."

Liz looked at her. Aside from a postcard here and there, and a few sporadic holiday cards that revealed nothing, she'd lost touch with Myra over the years. But her ex-maid-of-honor treated her as graciously as if they'd spoken daily.

Myra rummaged through her fringed, black purse and offered her a piece of fruit-flavored candy. *A Lifesavers moment.* Liz laughed and accepted the offering.

"Come on, Liz, I know if you could tell me, you would. Anyway, it really doesn't matter why you came back. What does is that you did." She wrinkled her nose. "Did that make any sense?"

"More sense than you know." A burst of gratitude warmed Liz's heart. Myra had taken her in hand the minute her mother had plopped her on her grandmother's doorstep. The outgoing woman before her had also been a friendly girl and she'd made Liz participate in kiddy, then teenage, social life, such as it was in Manchester County. If not for her, Liz would have set up shop at Gran's until summer vacation was over. Just like she shut herself in her new bedrooms whenever her mother dragged her from town to town, apartment to apartment. Sunny Braden could never much figure out her daughter. The way she saw it, her frequent moves opened up a whole new world of opportunity for the girl. Instead, Liz had always felt shut out. And so very, very alone.

She cleared her throat. "If it makes any difference, you are the best friend I ever had."

"Same here."

For a long, quiet moment, neither said anything. Then a grin enlivened Myra's attractive, uneven features and she leaned back in the booth. "Besides, now that you're back, I can take this trip Harvey has planned for us without worrying about leaving Bo and Ruth shorthanded."

"I knew there was an ulterior motive," Liz said wryly. It wasn't likely that Richard would come to his senses before the weekend. And the banks would be closed for the coming holiday anyway....

Myra must have taken her prolonged silence as reluctance. She said quickly, "Well, you said you wanted to keep busy. With me gone, you'll be that and more, especially with the July fourth festivities. You are going to help with Ruth's booth, right?"

Ruth's booth. With the busyness of the morning, Liz had nearly forgotten about the food booth Ruth and Bo always manned at any holiday or county event. She twisted her lips.

"Have you known anybody to say no to Ruth and have it stick?" she asked. "Enough of that. I want to know where you and Harvey are going. Have you decided?"

During mini-breaks throughout the day, Liz had had Myra fill her in on the past seven years. The chitchat let her find out about what her friend had been doing, and it also saved her from having to talk about the comical mess that was her own life.

Myra had told her she'd opened her own flower shop a few years ago only to watch it slide into debt under the weight of Manchester's weak economy. The only businesses that unfailingly survived in the small town were the general store, a nearby bar, Ezra's gas station and the diner. Even the dead went to an outside mortuary for final arrangements.

Liz had learned Harvey was her on-again, off-again boyfriend of the past year or so. He was from the neighboring county, and from what Liz could surmise, he was a bit of a rebel with his Harley and unplanned trips arranged to escape small-town life for a short stretch.

"Don't know where we're going this time," Myra finally said. "He should be here in a few minutes. We'll probably just jump onto that Harley of his and ride."

"Harvey and his Harley. Ingredients of every girl's dream."

"Maybe not yours," Myra said easily. "But definitely mine."

"So why don't you marry him?" Liz eyed her.

She shrugged. "He hasn't asked."

Liz choked on her response. Myra handed her a previous customer's half-empty glass of water.

"I'm joking," Myra said with a laugh. "You know, you don't fool me with those saucy smiles and zinging remarks of yours, Liz. You're as uptight as ever. While I'm gone you should really have a little fun. You look like you could use some." She gestured over her shoulder. "Why don't you take advantage of what life has to offer? Especially that prize customer of yours."

Liz's throat tightened. "Mitch doesn't tip well enough to be a prize customer."

"He always leaves me good ones." Myra's silver bracelets jangled as she pushed all five of them up her forearm.

"You're probably saying I should have some fun with Mitch because of this stupid bet."

"Don't put that one on me. You got yourself into that jumble all by your lonesome."

Liz looked up. "Speaking of which, who did *you* put your money on, Myra? Me or...him?"

"Hmm?" Liz watched Myra pretend an interest in putting back together the dismembered cherub scattered across the table.

Liz kept an eyebrow raised, noticing that the subject of their conversation had gone quiet as well.

"Okay. Let's put it this way, Elizabeth Braden. I still have hopes for you."

Myra had bet against her. "I can't believe you!"

"Yeah, well, believe it. While you and Mitch may have had a run at it before and failed, there's not a single reason why you can't have a little fun with him now. The type of fun that involves sheets, preferably of the silk variety. You know, at least until things settle down in Boston and you can get on with your plans."

If only her plans extended beyond waiting for Richard to calm down, maybe she'd feel better. Truth was, her plans' well was currently empty. And she didn't need help imagining that fun with Mitch would involve silk sheets. She cleared her throat. "This from a woman who dates a man named Harvey with a Harley."

"At least I have a man I want to run away with, not from."

Through the tall glass windows that looked out over manicured Main Street, Liz watched someone who could only be Harvey pull up on a chopper. His black hair was a tangled mass around his stern features, the tattoo of a skull vividly displayed on the fist-size muscle of his right arm. His dark attire matched Myra's, the exceptions being a red bandanna tied loosely around his tanned neck and the absence of a bra strap.

She gasped. "My God, Myra! If there was ever anyone to run from."

Myra quickly hugged her. "The tattoo washes off with soap and water and Harvey's an accountant in his day job."

"Call if you need anything, okay? Like if Harvey leaves you stranded out in the middle of nowhere with a hefty bar bill."

Myra laughed. "I will."

Liz stood and dragged the pile of plates to the edge of the table. "Oh, and about that bet, Myra." She smiled. "You're going to lose every stinking penny."

4

THAT FRIDAY at the Fourth of July county fair, Liz leaned against the food booth she was helping to man and drew in a deep, satisfying breath. There was nothing quite like the smells of sunshine, popcorn and cotton candy. Not to mention the aromas that wafted up from the table before her. She reached over and drew her fingertip across the bottom of the barbecue rib pan, ignoring the wobble of the table as she stuck her finger into her mouth.

She briefly closed her eyes, only to throw them open again when an enticing vision of Mitch emerged front and center. She dragged her finger from between her lips. She was beginning to suspect an image of him was forever etched into the backs of her eyelids. Even last night, when she'd tried to write an apologetic letter to Richard, thoughts of Mitch had distracted her. "Dear Richard, I know you don't know where I am, but rest assured I'm in good hands...." Then for the next ten minutes she'd thought about Mitch's hands and the many things she wanted him to do with them.

She'd plodded on. "I'm sorry for popping you in the nose. I'm not usually a physical person, but since I've gotten into town, all I can think about is getting even more physical...with Mitch...."

She'd crumpled at least eight such drafts before giving up on the endeavor entirely.

She shifted uneasily, and the table lurched.

"Oh no," Liz said under her breath, fastening a death grip on the corner as the back leg gave out.

She'd seen it coming since she'd set up for the three-day event hours earlier. Watched the wobbles when people bumped the front of the booth. The teeters when she and Ruth busily served ribs, potato salad, pork and beans and French fries to the harried lunch crowd. But the table hadn't given out then. Oh, no. It had to wait until Bo and Ruth had taken advantage of the present lull in customers to check out what else was going on around the fairgrounds. Until she was alone. Until, once again, thoughts of Mitch had completely distracted her.

The afternoon sun beat down on Liz's head, overheating her skin and dappling the leftover food spread across the tabletop. She leaned back, trying to get a look at the damage under the table.

"Need some help?"

Speak of the devil.

Mitch stood a few feet away, arms folded across his chest, his cowboy boots solidly planted on the hard dirt of the pathway. Liz nearly lost her grip—literally and figuratively. Damn, but the man had a way of chasing every thought, every intention from her mind.

She glanced up at him. "Depends on what it's going to cost me."

He grinned that maddening grin. "At this point, I think I can afford to throw you a freebie."

The corner she held dipped an inch and the food platters clattered ominously. "Are you going to help me get this leg back under the table now, or are you waiting to surprise me on my birthday?"

He uncrossed his arms. "It's my mission in life to help you with your legs, angel." He lazily dropped his gaze to where her khaki shorts ended and her tanned skin began. She'd bought a few things the day before with her first check, not that it mattered. The heat in his gaze made her feel completely naked, or at least made her yearn to be.

"Mitch McCoy, in two seconds everything Ruth and I spent two days making is going to end up on the ground. Now are you going to help me or not?"

He narrowed the distance between them, then knelt down and propped the table leg up. His forearm brushed against her bare calf. A delicious shiver shimmied up the back of her leg.

"Sorry," he murmured.

Scooting what few inches she could away from him, she tested the repair work, then released her grip. "You can get up now, Mitch."

"Hmmm...I like the view better from down here."

"I bet you do." Liz admired the way the sun reflected off his brown hair, livening the fair highlights, the wind teasing the thick, soft strands. She wanted to tunnel her fingers through it and tug that grinning mouth of his to hers. "But if you don't get up now, you're the one who's going to need help fixing one of your legs."

With a quiet chuckle, he rose to his feet. Liz swallowed hard, trying to determine whether or not he'd grown taller since the last time she saw him.

"Are you threatening bodily harm, Lizzie?"

"Uh-huh."

His brows lifted skeptically. "Not a particularly wise thing to do considering the trouble you're already in."

For the first time since she'd seen him standing backlit by the sun, she felt like smiling. And did.

"Okay, this time I'll bite. The circumstances surrounding my return are eating you alive, aren't they?"

It was satisfying to watch him cross his arms defensively.

"I don't particularly like the imagery associated with what you just said, but, yeah, I'll admit I'm a little curious."

"A little?"

"A little." He stood his ground.

"Good." She bent over and repositioned the ribs that had slid slightly when the table gave out.

"Is that it?" Mitch asked, coming to stand close. Too close.

She shrugged, though the last thing she felt was unaffected by his nearness. He was so...big. "Given your former occupations, I've no doubt you've already checked with the Virginia and Massachusetts authorities. And since you haven't said anything, I trust both checks came back clean."

"Should they have?"

"I'll let you be the one to figure that out." Kneeling down, she opened the portable refrigerator and took out a bowl of potato salad. "Want some?"

"No, thanks."

Picking up a plastic fork, she took a healthy bite of the blessedly cold food, though she suspected a freezer full of ice cubes wouldn't be enough to cool her off. And her condition had nothing to do with the summer sun. "Are you sure? Ruth really outdid herself this time."

He fairly growled. "I don't want any damn potato salad, Liz."

Sucking on the end of the fork, she watched him. She was really getting to him, wasn't she? Which was good. Because he got to her in a way she couldn't begin to fathom.

"Hey, Mitch."

Liz watched Mitch's brother, Jake McCoy, step up to the booth. Seeing as she'd been back for almost a week, she'd expected to run into more McCoys by now. She knew Marc was off on his honeymoon, but where were Connor and David? Around five years older than Mitch, Jake had always been the quietest of the brothers. Darker, more intense, he reminded her somewhat of the actor Jeff Goldblum.

"How are you, Elizabeth?"

She smiled at his formality. She couldn't remember one time when he'd called her Liz. "Fine. And you, Jake? I have to say, you're looking as good as ever."

She watched the tips of his ears redden, but little else betrayed what he was feeling. "Fine. I'm fine." He turned his attention toward Mitch, who looked anything but fine. "Where's Pops?"

Mitch grimaced. "He's not at the house?"

"No."

"Then, I don't know where he is. I haven't seen a whole lot of him myself lately."

Jake raised a brow. "Okay. Guess I'll catch up with him later."

Jake nodded at Liz, started to walk away, then hesitated. "I like how the place is coming along, Mitch."

Mitch jammed his fingers through his hair. "Thanks."

"Let me know if you need any more help."

"Sure."

Liz's gaze trailed to Mitch after Jake had disappeared down the fairway. "Everything all right with your father?"

"What? Yeah, sure, Pops is fine. But he isn't the one on my mind right now."

"Oh, now I know what you're worried about," she said jokingly. "It's the bet, isn't it?"

Again, he stepped closer. Liz backed up, her body on alert.

"No, angel, I'm talking about something entirely different."

Her throat grew dry. "Mind telling me what?"

"Well..." He scraped a rough fingertip along the cotton strap over her right shoulder. "Actually, it has to do with you telling me something I've been waiting seven years to hear."

The ground shifted beneath Liz's feet. She didn't have to ask him what that something was. She knew.

"Why did you leave me, Liz?"

In direct contrast to his chilly tone, his finger slid from the cotton to her bare shoulder, searing her flesh. A slight shift and his hand would rest over her breast. Oh, how she wanted to feel him there, cupping her, testing the weight in his palm.

She quickly moistened her lips and searched his eyes. The teasing there surprised her. She would have thought he'd be a little more serious when he broached the subject. As it was, he acted as if their conversation concerned nothing more than the color of her tank top.

"You know why," she whispered.

His gaze raked her face. "I do?"

"Yes...no...you know what I mean."

He slowly shook his head. "No, Liz, I can't say as I do." He suddenly shoved his hands into his jeans pockets and shifted his weight from one boot to the other. "Tell me, is the reason you left Boston the same reason you left me?" He held her gaze with a potency that had her mesmerized.

Liz searched his face, learning the new shadows of hurt and disappointment that lurked there. She wanted to reach out to smooth away the wrinkle of his dark brow and coax back the humor that made his eyes twinkle. But she didn't. The silence that clanked down around them wouldn't allow it. There was no room for soothing, for jokes. Their conversation had moved to more serious ground and now she would just have to stand on it. She fought to keep her gaze locked with his.

"No. The choice I made now," she said carefully, quietly,

trying to respond in a way that made sense, "is nothing like the choice I made seven years ago."

The pain that shadowed his face turned into a grimace. "You know, Liz, you've always been about as clear as a muddy river." He cursed under his breath. "What did you expect from me when you came back? That I would have forgiven you for something I can't begin to understand?"

"I don't expect anything from you, Mitch. You asked me if the choices I made were similar, and I gave you an answer." She clasped her fingers around her opposite arm. "Now if you want to talk about choices, then let's talk about the ones you gave me when I asked to postpone our ceremony."

"A request you made on the day of our wedding."

"Yes, on the day of our wedding." She caught herself rubbing her arm and dropped her hand. "What choices did you give me then, Mitch?"

He was silent, so she provided the answer for him. *"Either you marry me now, Liz, or you leave me and Manchester forever."*

She didn't need to remind him that she'd never been good with ultimatums. She'd spent her entire childhood waiting for that moment in time when she'd have control over her life. When she was no longer at the mercy of her mother's constant restlessness. When she was the one calling the shots. And his response...well, it had threatened that control. Sure, she'd known he'd said the words out of anger. But the moment they were out, they were out, hanging between them in large, bold, capital letters. It didn't matter that he didn't mean them, or that she'd loved him more than anything. The whole dynamic of their relationship had changed in that one moment. And that was something Liz couldn't live with. If she had stayed...well, she hadn't, had she?

Long minutes passed, then Mitch finally cleared his throat. "That doesn't explain why you asked for the postponement," he said.

"You didn't seem too interested in knowing why then," she said. She'd asked for the postponement because she was petrified. Terrified that she might not be the right woman for Mitch. Paralyzed with dread that she didn't belong.

She shook off her uneasiness, surprised to find those emotions remained even now.

Which was dumb, because they had both done what they had to.

"That was a long time ago, Mitch. Been there, done that, bought the T-shirt. No amount of talking about it now is going to change things, so why even bother?" She tucked her hair behind her ear, steadily holding his gaze. "You see the world one way. I see it another. We're just not suited for each other. Not for a kiss, not for a date, not for forever. Don't ask for any further explanation than that, because I don't think I can be any clearer than that without cussing."

Kids that had been hanging back neared the front of the booth, prodding at the food Liz had been putting away. They were laughing, but she couldn't concentrate on what they were saying.

"You've really thought about this, haven't you?" he asked, the sides of his mouth beginning to turn up.

She lifted a finger. "Now don't go making more of this—"

"Admit it, Liz, you've stayed awake nights fortifying your reasons not only for running out on me, but for not being with me now."

She felt as if he had stripped away her blanket on a cold winter's night. Or peeled back her clothes on a hot summer's day, just like this one. The contrast left a tantalizing tingle in her belly that refused to go away.

"Still, I want to remind you none of your reasons has anything to do with attraction."

Oh, he had her there. As far as the attraction angle went, she didn't think she could burn for a man more without self-combusting. Still, she said, "It takes more than attraction, Mitch."

"For marriage, yes, it does. For one date, how much more do you want? I'm not asking you to marry me again, angel."

"Date?" Of course, date. They were back to the cursed bet again. "Nice try, but you're going to have to do a whole helluva lot better than that if you hold out any hope of winning this bet."

He grasped her upper arms and hauled her closer. So much for not self-combusting. Flames seemed to lick over her skin from forehead to feet. "Forget the bet, Liz. I just think it fair for me to warn you: I want you. And, damn it, I'm not going to stop until I have you."

TWO DAYS LATER Liz sat at a pink booth, the squeak of her bare legs against plastic echoing through the empty diner. She absently tugged the hem of her silk shorts down farther to cover her skin. After three days manning the food booth at the fair, she, Bo and Ruth had finally closed up shop earlier tonight in preparation for the Fourth of July fireworks. Since everyone was at the fairgrounds anyway, the diner was closed, and Liz was left with nothing to do but think.

Not that there was much to think about. She propped her chin in her palm. Okay, so her plans for her future were basically a blank slate, but she couldn't do anything about that until Richard unfroze her assets. Something he had yet to do, as Sheila had told her the day before. Still, she couldn't seem to concentrate on anything other than what Mitch had said about wanting her, and about his obvious absence since making the declaration. Both things that had kept her up late into the night, yearning for an unnameable something that she was beginning to think no one but Mitch could give her.

She stared through the window next to her at the darkening sky. About a half mile down the road at the fairgrounds, the bright tail of a skyrocket heralded what would soon be the beginning of the fireworks display. Liz hadn't known she'd sighed until she heard the wistful sound break the silence of the empty diner.

Everyone would be at the fairgrounds now, stretching blankets out on the dewy grass, reaching into coolers for colas and beer, lighting sparklers for the kids, having fun that wouldn't end with the fireworks. She shifted, wincing when her skin peeled from the plastic again. *Fun*. She hadn't had much of that in recent years. If she were honest, aside from the brief snatches of promise the first few days in a new city brought, she hadn't had near the adventure she had sworn she'd have when she'd left Manchester.

First she'd gone to Cleveland, where she'd lived with her bohemian mother and taken some night school courses at a local college, earning her bachelor's in business. Then the harsh lake-effect winters had chased her from the bustling city to Chicago, which was laughable, because the winters had been even worse there, and the busy metropolis had certainly earned the title Windy City during the year she had stayed.

Next had come St. Louis and Philadelphia.

In the meantime, as a consultant she'd steadily moved up from helping small business and restaurant owners turn a healthy profit to signing large contracts with major industrial firms and service agencies.

Then there was Boston and her biggest contract yet with a centuries-old bank. Only, that contract had a handsome, charming male attached in the shape of a vice president named Richard Beschloss.

Liz absently gathered the brochures littering the table in front of her into a pile, feeling much as if she was gathering scattered playing cards. Only she had yet to find an ace in this deck. For days, she'd been toting around the pamphlets she'd picked up on her way to Manchester trying to figure out where she wanted to head next. Dallas, L.A., Seattle, Miami? She had solid contacts in each of the cities, contacts she could use to re-establish herself. And she could get letters of recommendation from nearly everyone she'd worked with. Except for Richard, of course. But none of the places had jumped out at her. Wherever she decided to head, she had enough capital to get herself up and running again—if she could ever regain access to her personal and business accounts in Boston, that is.

She'd never thought Richard Beschloss would be so vengeful.

She bent the corner of the brochure on Atlanta back and forth. Just before she had become engaged, a professional headhunter had approached her with a job opportunity in the southern city. The position would mean working for somebody else instead of herself, but the company was good, and job security was guaranteed.

A clang of metal drew her attention back to the well-lit street. Liz slid over the booth, closer to the window, immediately recognizing the red truck parked in front of the general store across the street. Mitch climbed out, leaving the door open only long enough for Goliath to jump out after him.

"Mitch McCoy, where in the hell have you been?" Liz murmured in the quiet of the diner.

It wasn't like him to drop a bombshell such as the one he had the other day, then disappear. Then again, did she really even know *what* he was like anymore? She was beginning to think she didn't.

Why wasn't he at the fairgrounds? And why in the world was he re-stocking the two vending machines that stood sentinel at either side of the entrance to the general store?

He lowered the tailgate of the truck, the dog barking and nipping at his heels.

"Down, Goliath," Mitch ordered, his voice drifting through the open diner door. He freed his right hand and scratched the dog behind one of his ears.

Goliath knocked him off balance. A few foil bags of chips slid from the box and scattered across the sidewalk. Mitch didn't even frown as he put the box down, gathered up the items, then used his keys to open the large, glass-fronted door of the first machine.

My, but he has a great pair of buns.

When she saw him like this—with several yards separating them and no curious onlookers around—Liz admitted she'd always liked looking at him. No, *like* wasn't the word. *Relished* was better. He had the type of body that commanded attention. Long, slender and solid. More than that, Mitch exuded a strength she wondered at. It was more than the tight fit of his T-shirts, the just-right shade of his faded jeans and his broken-in cowboy boots. It was the man himself. A man who never seemed flustered by anything. In fact he gave the impression he was quite pleased with himself and his life, even in moments when nobody was around to watch him.

Still, none of that explained why Mitch was stocking vending machines when he should be at the fairgrounds, settling in with the rest of the town for the fireworks display. She plucked at the brochure. He should be with a pretty, single woman, mapping out plans for starting a family. Living the life they had once planned to live.

An anxious sense of loneliness sank into Liz. She'd never much liked the "what if" game, but lately she'd found herself coming back to this one. What if she had stayed? What if she had never asked for the postponement, thus provoking his ultimatum? Compelling her to leave?

Goliath abruptly turned toward her and started barking. Liz was suddenly aware that she sat spotlighted in the empty diner, though it wouldn't surprise her one bit if Mitch had known she was there all along, ogling him. He shifted his head, noting her Lexus parked on the street, then stared right at her through the window. He offered up his devilish grin and her heart thudded. Liz tugged her gaze away from his and jerked the cover on the brochure on Atlanta open in front of her.

"What is it about you, Mitch, that won't let me chase you from my heart?" she muttered.

Goliath's nails clicked against the tiled floor and the sound of footsteps followed. Liz shivered, despite the sultry heat of the night.

She pulled her notepad closer and wrote down words that made absolutely no sense. Something cold and wet touched her calf and she jumped. She laughed at her own high sensitivity and bent to pet Goliath. "Come here, you big slobber puss. How did you get in here?" She cleared her throat and looked at Mitch where he stood near the door. "Oh. I didn't hear you come in."

Liar. Even if she hadn't heard or seen him, she'd have known he was nearby just by taking a deep breath of his warm, outdoorsy scent.

His eyes momentarily darkened, but his grin didn't waver.

Goliath's tail thumped against the side of the booth and Liz petted him again.

"Coffee sounds good right about now," Mitch said.

She poked a thumb toward the half pot she'd made a little earlier, still on the hot plate behind the counter. "I'm off duty." She gave the dog a final pat and turned back to her brochures. "Anyway, the diner's closed. Didn't you see the sign?"

He ignored her and walked toward the counter. He blew into a clean cup, filled it, then turned back. He took the seat across from her.

She glanced up from where she pretended to scour the brochures. "There are at least twenty other tables to sit at in this diner, Mitch."

"Yeah, but none of them have an angel sitting at them."

She plucked an ever-present cherub from its spring stand

and tossed it his way. "That's going to have to do, because I'm a little busy right now."

He picked up the cherub from his lap and tossed it back onto the table. "I can see that." He fingered a brochure, then drew it in his direction. He raised a dark brow. "Miami?"

She snatched back the brochure with a picture of a pink flamingo on the cover and stuffed it under the others. "Why aren't you at the fairgrounds with everybody else?"

His grin widened. "I have to say, Liz, your interest in my activities never ceases to amaze me."

At least she hadn't asked him where he'd been—which was just as well, because she had the sneaking suspicion he wouldn't tell her.

She scribbled on the notepad, overly aware of the way his gaze slid over her hair, face and neck like a caress. "Don't tell me. Your new career stocking vending machines is what's keeping you busy."

"Vending ma—" He apparently realized what she was talking about and chuckled. "I'm just looking after those for Klammer. He's on his yearly pilgrimage to Key West to see his old friend Ernest. Should be back sometime next week."

Liz straightened the strap of her silk tank that had slipped down over her shoulder. Her skin was hot to the touch and she wondered if she was as flushed as she felt. "Somebody ought to tell him Hemingway died over thirty years ago."

"I thought you did once."

She met his gaze and smiled. "Yeah, I guess I did. Not that it did any good if he's still going down there."

A loud boom reverberated through the night air. She turned toward the window to find the first of the fireworks shooting across the sky.

"I answered your question. How about you answer one of mine?" Mitch said.

"Depends on what it is."

"How come you're not at the fairgrounds?"

She peered under the table at Goliath, who had taken up residence on one of her feet. Her heart felt impossibly light— the sight, the circumstances, the company all too familiar. Of course, seven years ago Goliath had been little more than a few years old. She'd adopted him as a puppy from one of her neighbor's litters only to find out her grandmother had a violent allergic reaction to him every time he got within smelling distance. She looked at the grown dog now, grateful that Mitch had kept his promise to look after him.

She heated under his probing gaze, realizing he was waiting for an answer to his question. "I figured now was as good a time as any to get my plans together."

He ran his callused thumb over the rim of his cup. "Does that mean whoever you're running from has found you?"

She laughed. Trust him to remember something she'd said to bait him.

"No, it doesn't mean that," she murmured. "Besides, I didn't say I was running away from anybody. I said I needed to get away from someone. Big difference." She twirled the pencil in her fingers, cursing softly when it slipped from her grip and dropped to the floor. She bent to pick it up and bumped against Mitch's hand as he did the same thing from the other side of the table. A flush of awareness hastened up her arm and she slowly pulled her hand back, sitting up to take the pencil from him.

Mitch grinned at her mischievously. "So I take it you haven't noticed the strange guy in town then."

6

MITCH WATCHED LIZ closely for her response. Not so much as a batting eyelash gave away her thoughts.

When he'd spotted the fiftyish stranger in the late-model Chevy hanging around the fairgrounds two days ago, then on Main Street yesterday, he'd asked David to run a check on the plates through DCPD's central computers. It had come back as a rental out of Dulles airport. The youngest McCoy had asked if he wanted him to check further, to get the name and address on the rental contract, but Mitch had declined, deciding to use the information he had to get answers from Liz first.

Her hazel eyes seemed to challenge him. He wasn't going to get any more than he'd already gotten from her, which was precious little.

"What strange guy?" she asked. "I think everybody in this town is a bit strange."

She glanced through the window at her Lexus, and he followed her gaze. It was the first time he'd seen her drive it. Since she'd arrived, the car had sat under that damn tarp in her backyard and she'd been catching rides with Ruth into town. Why had she used it now? And why was she looking like it had been a mistake?

"What's the matter, Liz? You seem a bit jumpy tonight."

"Maybe it's because I've had one too many cups of coffee," she answered and rose from the booth. "But, what the heck, one more won't hurt."

He held up his half-empty cup and she ignored him. He put the cup back down and looked under the table to where Goliath shifted to sit on his foot instead of Liz's. Briefly, he wanted to nudge the little Judas away, but allowed him to settle. After all, the dog wasn't the only one who wanted to touch Liz. Only Mitch had much more than just her foot in mind.

His gaze strayed to her walking away from him. Her hips were lush and inviting under the thin silk of her peach-colored shorts. He told himself he should be glad she was wearing something other than those cut-offs and that Georgetown T-shirt, but he honestly could say that the curve-clinging silk was worse. It clung to her rounded bottom like a second skin when she walked, and seemed a lighted billboard advertising just how soft the flesh was that the material covered.

He didn't try to hide his interest in her figure as she walked back to the table with the coffeepot, surprising him by topping off his cup before filling her own. She put the pot on the table. He curved his fingers around her wrist, holding her in place.

"Tell me, is it really the coffee, Liz, or is it the company making you so nervous?" he murmured, his gaze sweeping her upturned face.

Her skin was cool and velvety under his callused fingertips. So cool he thought he might scorch her. A slow burn began deep in his groin.

She laughed a little too lightly, still standing next to the booth. "I've never been nervous in my life, Mitch McCoy. You know that."

"Maybe that was true of the old Elizabeth Braden," he said quietly, scraping his thumb against her wrist and down to the sensitive area of her palm. The movement of his rough skin over her lotion-soft hand felt incredibly provocative.

She shuddered and something answered inside him. He halted the movement of his thumb and formed his masking grin. "But this Liz—this new Liz—seems plenty nervous to me."

She tried to tug her wrist away, only serving to tighten his grip. Her breath came in shallow gasps, and he could feel her thundering pulse under his thumb.

"What? You don't really think you're the one making me nervous, do you, Mitch?"

He stared at a shiny, saffron lock of her hair swept against her tanned shoulder. Impulsively, he wanted to rake it back from her enchanting face.

"The thought had crossed my mind," he drawled.

"Well, you better let that thought just keep on going, because you don't have a thing to do with my being anxious. And I'm not saying I am anxious, by the way."

"Of course not," he readily agreed. "Anyway, if you were nervous, it could have as much to do with that stranger in town as it does with me, right?"

She narrowed her hazel eyes. "Is there really a stranger in town, or are you pulling my leg?"

"Oh, if I were pulling your leg, you'd know it, angel. Trust me."

She tried to tug her arm away again, catching him unaware. He tightened his grip and the movement had a reactive effect that hurled her directly into his lap. He stared at her startled expression. She wriggled against him. While the predicament wasn't one he had planned, one particular part of his body readily welcomed her lush bottom pressed against him—a physical response Liz didn't miss if her soft intake of breath was anything to go by. And he was betting it was.

"Well, nice of you to drop in so unexpectedly," he murmured, the sweet smell of wild cherries filling his senses.

She wriggled to free herself from his grasp, serving only to elicit a groan from his suddenly raw throat.

He encircled her waist with his arms, bumping the table in the process, nearly spilling his coffee. "Would you stop struggling a minute before you end up doing some serious damage?"

"I'm not going to stop until you let me go."

Realizing this wasn't fun and games anymore, he released his grip. While her being planted in his lap had been an accident, he could see where she might view it differently given his manipulative behavior lately. Awareness surged through him like an express steam-engine with one destination, but he would never physically press himself on her. No, she was going to be the one coming to him. Willingly. Hungrily.

She stopped struggling, her hazel eyes all sexy and warm.

"What is it?" he murmured. "You're free to go. So go."

She stayed right where she was.

His gaze flicked over her flushed face. The damn woman confused him more than she ever had. Who else but Liz would fight like a spitfire to free herself, then stay as if to spite him? Didn't she realize what she was doing to him? He swallowed, his gaze skimming her pink lips. Or maybe she knew exactly what she was doing and he had just opened a wide passage for her to exact her own brand of revenge.

"Funny, but, um...I don't want to go anymore," she murmured.

An emotion stronger than any he'd ever experienced quaked through him. "I'm warning you, Liz. If you don't get up right now, I won't be held responsible for my actions."

Her teasing little smile made his mouth water. "Aren't those usually my words?" She lifted a hand and ran her fingertip along the ridge of his jaw. "Looks like the tables have turned, haven't they?"

"Speaking of tables, you realize you're two seconds away from ending up flat against the top of this one, don't you?"

"Yes, well, maybe it's about time we ended up horizontal together somewhere, isn't it?"

Heat blasted through his veins. For the second time, Liz was kissing him. But where the first one in her house had been tauntingly carnal, her exploration now was haltingly sweet, reminding him of stolen kisses when they were teenagers. A groan clogged his throat and he moved his hands from where they rested at his sides so he could tunnel his fingers in her golden hair. He molded her mouth against his, drawing from her all the promises that had gone unfulfilled, glimpsing all they could have had if only he hadn't chased her away.

That glaring truth caused a second groan to follow the first. Even as he parted her lips and gained access to the rich depths of her mouth, he knew that's what he'd done: he had chased the only woman he'd ever cared for from his life.

Pushing the coffee cups out of the way, he lifted her so her bottom sat on the table. With a shaking hand, he nudged her thighs apart and slid his fingers up the leg of her shorts. His knuckles brushed against the damp front of her panties. She whimpered, kissing him harder as she moved her hips closer. He placed a stilling hand against her stomach, then began working the hem of her silk tank top up until her matching silk bra was exposed.

He caught his breath. No one could quite fill a bra the way Liz could. Not too big, not too small, the supple flesh curved just so over the top of the cups, tempting his mouth. He ran his tongue slowly across one slope, dipped it into the shallow valley, then trailed it across the other, before fastening his lips over her right nipple.

Her shuddering response edged up his own need. The silk of her bra was soft, the nipple beneath hard and round. He pulled at it through the material. She restlessly moved her hands through his hair, holding him there, aiding him when he moved to lavish attention on the other breast, leaving a round wet spot in his wake.

She tasted so good…so damn right.

He skimmed his fingers down her sides, over her thighs, then slipped them again under the hem of her shorts. She went completely still, her heartbeat a rapid staccato against his ear. He closed his eyes, savoring the amplified quiet of the moment. Enjoying the sweet anticipation. Then he gently probed her engorged flesh and dipped the tip of his fingers in her dripping heat.

Her moan, deep and soft, wove its way around him.

"Oh, how I want you," he ground out, his erection pressing painfully against his jeans.

Her eyes, half-lidded and drugged, stared at him. "Then take me, McCoy."

He bolted from the booth toward the row of lights near the kitchen door while she yanked closed the caf-style curtains at the windows. Within seconds, the diner was dark, the door closed, and he had her sprawled across the top of the table. She ripped at his T-shirt and the buttons on his jeans. He tugged off his boots, then her tank top, shorts and panties.

She was the most beautiful thing he'd ever seen.

In the golden light shining in from the top of the windows, her skin shimmered richer than the silk he'd taken off her. Her breasts were two peaks that rose and fell as her breath quickened, topped with pale, engorged nipples. He slid his hands up from her waist and cupped the firm globes, running his thumbs over the puckered nipples, wondering at their hardness. He hungrily lowered his mouth to capture first one, then the other, afraid he'd never be able to kiss them enough to make up for the past seven years. Afraid that if he didn't take her now, he'd never have the chance again.

Liz alternated between shoving his jeans down his hips, then bracing herself against the table, the restless sounds she made driving him onward. Finally, his jeans fell to the floor and he stepped out of them, stopping only long enough to get the condom from his wallet before again positioning himself between her thighs.

The sight of him poised just so against the pale tangle of curls between her legs made him pause. His breathing stopped. His heart beat loudly in his ears. How many times had they made it this far before only to pull back? One or the other of them regaining control of their actions and stopping before things went too far?

His gaze swept up to her face. The need, raw and undiluted, that shone in her eyes told him there would be no turning back now. There was no wedding night to wait for. No preconceived ideas on just how, exactly, their first time should play out. Not a champagne glass, a heart-shaped bed, or red satin sheets in sight. Only her, him and their pure, physical need for each other.

He hadn't realized he'd closed his eyes until he felt her fingers slide the condom over his pulsating shaft, then settle the tip between her soft folds of flesh. She leaned her hands far back on the table, then thrust forward, surrounding him with her slick, tight flesh, hungrily drawing him in. A groan gathered in the back of his throat as he grasped her hips, holding her still, holding her near. He stayed like that for a long moment, ignoring her quiet pleas. He'd waited too damn long for this. He intended to make it last.

Slowly, he counted backward. Ten...nine...eight...

Her sleek muscles flexed around him. The groan ripped from him and he thrust deeply into her, feeling her expand to accommodate him, feeling himself hardening all the more.

He'd never wanted a woman more than he wanted Liz Braden right now.

She wriggled free from his grasp and wound her legs around his waist. He nearly died right then and there when she lifted her hips with the sheer strength of those same legs and ground against him needfully. His ears were filled with her soulful moans, his body surrounded by her sweet, sweet flesh.

He thrust into her once. Then again. And again and again. Each and every move only making him want to move more. Over and over. Harder. Deeper.

Grabbing him by the shoulders, Liz lifted herself from the table until only his thighs rested against the side, the shift allowing him to go deeper still. He wrapped his arms around her silken body, flattening her breasts against his hair-peppered chest, squeezing her luscious rear with his hands. Then he slid his fingers between her legs from behind until he felt her slippery wetness, felt where they were joined.

His climax seemed to spiral up and up from the soles of his feet, gaining speed, gaining potency, until he exploded into her with his own unique brand of fireworks. Her own orgasm followed and she gripped his shoulders for dear life.

He stood like that for what seemed like forever—buried in her sleek flesh, his legs locked, his fingers clutching her soft bottom, her body quivering against his. She lifted her head from where she'd thrown it back. He kissed her, passionately, then dragged his mouth across her temple to push the damp wisps of hair back there.

Their eyes met.

In the dim light from the streetlamps outside the window, he read in her eyes everything he felt. Wonder. Amazement. Hunger. A seemingly insatiable hunger that even now had him hardening inside her again.

He claimed her swollen mouth with his own, moving his hands to rest on either side of her satiny neck as she clutched his shoulders. He gave himself over to the squall of agitated emotions swirling in his chest, punctuated by the boom of distant firecrackers in the warm night.

Liz slowed their kiss, then nipped at his bottom lip, catching it between her slightly crooked white teeth, her hazel eyes holding him transfixed. The affectionate gesture reminded him too much of the past. Of tortuous moments looking at her and fearing he could never have her. Of feeling she wasn't a woman of flesh and bone, a person he could hold on to, but a wild exotic butterfly constantly soaring just beyond his reach. A butterfly whose ceaselessly flapping wings did the most amazing things to his insides. A butterfly that fled when he tried to catch her with his net.

Liz broke off the kiss, her breath coming in quick gasps. She smiled and rested her forehead against his.

"You're...I'm...that was...incredible," she whispered, her tongue dipping out to moisten her just-kissed lips.

"Yes, I'd say that was worth seven years of absent foreplay," he managed to push from his raw throat.

She flexed her leg muscles around his waist, causing the tightening of other muscles as well. He groaned. She laughed, a low, raspy sound that affected him as much as her nearness.

"Mitch, tell me, why didn't you ever...well, why hadn't..."

He tilted his head back to get a better look at her. Now that they'd finally made love she was even more enchanting...and just as elusive. And he felt himself being reintroduced to the ripping, consuming, adolescent love he'd always felt for her.

Aw, hell.

"What?" he asked. Telling himself he should put her down, push her away. But unable to do either.

"Never mind," she said quietly, to his relief.

The shrill ring of the phone sliced through the needy cloud

accumulating around them again. But instead of moving to free herself, Liz burrowed further into his chest.

Goliath scratched the door from the kitchen where Mitch had shut him in.

"Um, don't you think you should get that?" he asked, suddenly urgent to escape the vacuum-like suck of the past. Because, even as her familiar scent tempted his nose, inviting him to breathe her in, he suspected that what had just happened between them had little or nothing to do with the present. He was afraid their lovemaking had come as a result of completing something they'd never had.

She stiffened in his arms, and he reluctantly lowered her to the floor, wondering if she was thinking the same as he was. The damnable thing about the whole situation was that he really didn't want to let her go. Not to move away from him. Not to get the phone. Not to leave Manchester.

He grimaced as he reached for his jeans. So much for casual sex.

EVERY INCH of Liz's skin tingled, every nerve ending sang as she quickly threw her clothes on, then made her unsteady legs carry her to the cash register and the phone. Leaning against the glass-topped case, she pushed her tousled hair back from her face and groped for the receiver. She noticed a dark spot on her tank top and pulled it away from her torso to follow the stain onto her shorts. A glance at the table told her it must be coffee. The new shorts set was ruined, but she couldn't seem to make herself care.

"Hello?" she croaked, then cleared her throat, looking to where Mitch had gotten dressed and turned on the lights. He stepped behind the counter and scooped ice into a glass and filled it with water.

Static crackled over the telephone line. "Hello?" she said again, more clearly. "Bo and Ruth's Paradise Diner."

"Liz, is that you? Thank God you're there. When I didn't see you at the fairgrounds, I hoped you might be at the diner...."

The connection was bad, but Liz thought she made out Ruth's voice. "Ruth? What's the matter?"

"The matter? Well, let's see, aside from the fact that this call is being transmitted through the state police over a radio because I'm in the back of an ambulance heading for D.C., everything's just peachy."

Liz's knees went weak for a second time. "Ambulance? My God, what's happened?"

There was a brief moment of silence. Liz guessed Ruth was trying to pull herself together, an image that was hard to form because Ruth was the most together person she knew. Something was very wrong.

"Bo had a mild heart attack, Liz. The paramedics say it's not serious. He must have just tired himself out this past weekend, what with the festivities and all...."

Liz felt Mitch's hands on her arms and she automatically leaned into him. He tightened his grip.

"What is it?" he asked quietly.

Liz covered the mouthpiece with her hand. "It's Bo...he's had a heart attack."

His expression held all the concern she felt.

Ruth's voice continued in her ear, sounding more like herself than she did a moment ago. "I told the big oaf he needed to start watching his diet, more vegetables and less of that artery-clogging stuff. But did he listen? No. He wears that belly of his like it's some kind of trophy he's won."

Liz smiled shakily, hearing the sound of a man's voice in the background.

"Would you just shush a minute and let the man do his job," Ruth said. Relief flushed through Liz's frazzled mind. "That's Bo." Ruth confirmed her suspicion. "He's giving the paramedic a hard time. Big surprise. Look, I can't talk long, but I wanted to let you know they're probably going to keep Bo at the hospital in the city for a couple of days, you know, for observation. And I—"

"—want to stay with him," Liz finished for her. "Of course you do. Don't worry. I'll look after the diner." She briefly bit her lip, surprised to find herself near tears. "Is there anything else you need?"

Ruth told her no, that she was having somebody else look into getting them a change of clothes, then Liz quickly told her to give Bo their love. She didn't catch her mistake until Ruth paused.

"Who's *our*?" the older woman asked.

"Our?"

"You said, 'Give Bo *our* love,'" she pressed. "Is there somebody there with you? It's Mitch, isn't it?"

She glanced at the man next to her.

"Mitch? Of course he's not here. I said 'our' in terms of the whole town. As in, give Bo Manchester's love." Liz cringed, afraid she was sounding as crazy as the town's other occupants. Mitch's chuckle didn't help matters much, either. She elbowed him in the ribs.

"Uh-huh," Ruth said, unconvinced. "You're a terrible liar, Liz. Anyway, tell your company that I fully expect him to help you out while Bo and I are gone."

"I'll tell him whenever I see him next. Goodbye, Ruth," Liz said firmly. "Call me from the hospital once Bo's settled in."

She quickly hung up the phone and turned around—and put herself squarely back in the cradle of Mitch's arms.

"He's going to be okay, I take it?" he asked, his gaze scraping her heated cheeks.

"Um...he was arguing with the paramedics, so I think that's a pretty good sign."

Mitch chuckled. "Bo will probably argue with St. Peter."

Liz cleared her throat, unsure how she felt after everything that had happened tonight. She glanced over his shoulder to where Goliath again slept under the table. "Looks like you're going to have to carry him out of here."

The night was silent and Liz realized the fireworks display must have ended. Everybody would be heading home soon, a good number of them passing through town with a clear view inside the diner. She suddenly realized that anyone passing too close to the windows might have seen them....

"So, what time should I be here to help you open up in the morning?" he asked, his gaze fastened to her mouth.

"Time?"

He grinned. "I take it from your side of the conversation that Ruth had something she wanted you to pass on to me. I'm assuming it was to help you out with the diner."

Liz forced her attention away from him and his sexy green eyes. "Yes, in fact she did. But you don't have to help. You already have enough to do, what with your private investigating...the vending machines...and..." She stared at him. Lord help her, but she wanted to push him back to that table and continue acquainting herself with his body.

"Is six okay?" he asked, ignoring her protests.

"Six?" she echoed, realizing she was repeating his words a lot.

"Five?"

"No, no. Six is fine."

He hesitated. "Then I guess I'll see you at six."

"Yeah, six. You want me to swing by to pick you up?"

His brow budged upward.

"You know, since it's on my way and everything. No sense both of us driving in separately."

"Sure. Why don't you pick me up."

She eyed his mouth, fervently wishing he would kiss her again. And scared to death that he wouldn't. Instead, he let loose a low whistle and Goliath slowly scrambled to his feet, stopping for a goodnight pet from Liz before sauntering out the open diner door with Mitch.

MITCH SAT in the McCoy kitchen alone, realizing after a half hour he hadn't turned on the lights. If anything was capable of putting his libido in check, the news about Bo should have been it. But not even his concern for a man who had pretty much been a constant fixture in his life could stop him from thinking about what had passed between him and Liz at the diner. His pulse still throbbed a steady rhythm, and he swore he could still taste her sweet flavor on his tongue. In the back of his mind ever since she'd driven back into town was his fear that things would be as good between them now as they were back then. Trouble was, he'd discovered that things were even better.

Better? Hell, he'd had a hard time not peeling those silk shorts from her hips and taking her all over again.

The sound of truck tires on the gravel drive snapped his attention toward the door. Pops. He'd probably been at the fairgrounds for the fireworks display and was just now coming home. Mitch quickly switched on the lights, then sat back down at the table just as the door opened.

"Hey there," Connor said as he walked in, followed by what appeared to be the entire McCoy clan, minus Marc, still honeymooning with his new bride. Lucky Marc.

Mitch stifled a groan, warily eyeing his brothers and father. "Hey, yourself."

David walked to the refrigerator and pulled out beers one by one. Jake took the seat across from Mitch and accepted his along with a glass. He poured the golden liquid inside. "I didn't see you at the fairgrounds tonight, Mitch," he said almost accusingly.

Mitch refused the bottle David offered as the rest of them

took their regular seats around the table. "Maybe that's because I wasn't there." Which had probably been a mistake. In a town as small as Manchester, often a person's absence was more worthy of comment than his appearance.

Pops popped the tab on a soda. "Then you probably didn't hear what happened to Bo."

"Actually," Mitch said slowly, "I did hear. I'm, um, going to be taking over his responsibilities at the diner. You know, until he's well enough to come back."

The kitchen went silent—which was saying a lot, because when there were this many McCoys in the house, the place was never silent.

Mitch leaned back in his chair and absently patted Goliath. For the past week, he'd been dying for someone, anyone, to talk to about Liz, and what was going on. Now that he had the chance, he wanted to be alone.

Didn't make a lick of sense. Then again, sense seemed to have flown out of town the instant that Liz drove in.

Jake leaned his forearms on the table. Wearing a crisply pressed oxford shirt and khakis, he was the best dressed of them. He always was. "Where'd you get the news? Somebody call you here?"

Mitch's hand stilled on Goliath's head. Even if the house was full of men in law enforcement, it didn't take a badge to figure out that something was going on here. "Nope. I happened to be at the diner when Ruth called."

David took a long pull from his bottle. "Hey, what's this, the third degree? Who cares who heard what when?"

Pops agreed, "I second that."

Mitch snapped his head up. In his father's eyes he saw recognition and understanding, which only confirmed his suspicion that there was more going on here than casual conversation.

Jake was like a bulldog with a rabbit caught in his teeth though. "Was Liz there with you?"

There it was. The reason for this midnight showdown in the McCoy kitchen.

Momentarily, Mitch empathized with every illegal alien in the country. If this was the way Jake, the INS agent, questioned his own brother, he shuddered to think what he did with total strangers who had actually broken a law.

Then again, maybe *he* had broken a law. One right out of the Jake McCoy Rules of Conduct Handbook. *Thou shalt not fraternize with those who have left you standing at the altar.* He grimaced. That sucker was probably as thick as the D.C. public phone book.

Connor nearly choked on his beer. "Liz? Did you just say Liz?" David shrugged, obviously as in the dark as he was. No one else answered him. "We're not talking little Lizzie Braden here, are we? She left eons ago, didn't she? The day—" His words abruptly cut off.

Connor merely swore succinctly.

Pops leaned back in his chair, the wooden creak serving to heighten the tension. "How's she doing, Mitch?"

He jammed his fingers through his hair and let loose a gusty sigh. "Fine. She's doing fine, Pops."

Jake muttered, "She ought to be tarred and feathered for what she did to you."

Tarred and feathered? Mitch nearly laughed at the absurdity of the situation. He figured it was good Jake hadn't been the one to cross paths with Liz the night she rolled into town. He had a feeling she'd still be in the local lockup.

"Self-imposed exile not enough for you, eh, Jake?" Pops said, his blue eyes throwing mischievous sparks.

Jake sat back in his chair and cracked his own smile. "It's a start."

The tightness in Mitch's neck eased a bit. Perhaps it was

his own frustration brought on by the night's earlier events that had him raring for a confrontation, purposely misreading his brother's intentions. Oddly enough, he didn't want his pound of flesh from Liz for walking out on him. He wanted all her delectable flesh to do with as he pleased.

His remaining tension shifted to other parts of his anatomy.

"So Liz is back, huh?" David said, shaking his head in wonder. "She still as much of a looker as she was back then?"

Connor chuckled. "If life was fair, she'd weigh five hundred pounds and look like Attila the Hun."

Mitch laughed. Not because of what Connor had said so much as the realization that he'd likely still want Liz no matter what she weighed or looked like.

"Well, we all know life is not fair," Jake said with a long-suffering sigh. "The damn girl is as gorgeous as ever."

Mitch hiked a brow. "I didn't know you noticed things like that, Jake."

"Hey, I notice a whole lot more than you guys give me credit for." He sat a little straighter.

David slapped him heartily on the back. "I can vouch for that. He's a pain in the ass when we go out together in D.C. Can't keep a conversation going for more than a minute without his attention wondering to the latest girl walking by." He shook his head. "The pisser is there seems to be something about that tall, dark and brooding bit that women go for, because they're all over him."

Connor set his bottle onto the table with a thud. "I think it's more of the hard-to-get thing, myself. Women always want what they can't have."

Mitch watched Jake closely. Was it him, or were his brother's ears growing a little red at the tips?

But it was Connor's comment that rang through his mind.

Women always want what they can't have. Could the same be said for men? He didn't like the looks of that dark mental road and reined in his thoughts.

Pops coughed. "You guys are as bad as a bunch of old women at a bridge game. Talking about each other's sex lives like that."

Mitch's gaze homed in on him. "Speaking of sex lives, yours seems to have picked up momentum recently."

His brothers' heads nearly snapped off as they turned toward their father. "Pops? Sex?" David fairly croaked.

Connor elbowed him hard, nearly forcing him off his chair. "Yeah, you know, that thing he did way back when to conceive your sorry butt."

"Who? What? Where? When?" Jake said without pause, glancing at Mitch when their father didn't answer.

Mitch shrugged. "Haven't been able to figure it out yet, and he's not giving up the info. Can't be anyone local, though, or else I'd have heard about it."

Pops waved the interest away, but his wide grin told Mitch that things must still be going well with his mysterious lady friend. "I'm not about to justify this line of questioning with a response. Did I say you were as bad as old women? I stand corrected. You're far worse."

David grinned. "Speaking of sex, has anybody heard from Marc and Mel? I'll bet they're having a lot of, um, *fun* on that cruise ship."

"I wouldn't be too sure," Mitch said, telling them Melanie had called the house the day before. "I guess there's been an incident or two involving motion sickness."

Pops sighed. "I told that boy it wasn't a good idea to take a pregnant woman on a boat, no matter how big."

"Marc's the one who's sick."

Everyone at the table erupted with laughter.

Pops started to get up from the table. "I think this is the point where I call it a night."

Mitch grinned. "'Night, Pops."

Jake stared at him. "You're not just going to let him leave without giving us some answers, are you?"

"What would you have us do, Jake? Tie him to his chair until he 'fesses up?"

"Not a bad idea."

Mitch grinned. "Yeah, right up there with the tarring and feathering suggestion."

"So I'm a little protective when it comes to family. Shoot me."

David got up and put his bottle away. "Don't tempt him. It may have been a while since Mitch has carried a gun, but I bet he can still beat the hell out of all of us at target practice."

Connor got up, too. "Yeah, well, maybe you should concentrate on your own sex life there, Jake, and keep your crooked nose out of everyone else's."

Absently, Jake reached up and ran his thumb and index finger down the length of his nose.

Connor stepped to Mitch and grasped his shoulder. "You do what you need to with Lizzie, ya hear? And if this guy gives you any trouble, just let me know. I'll set him straight."

David angled around Connor to look at Mitch. "Ditto for me."

"I'm heading back into the city. You coming, Jake?" Connor asked.

"Yeah, I'll be out in a minute."

Connor left the house, the slap of the screen door marking his departure. Mitch couldn't help thinking that Jake still had something to say, given the way his gaze rarely left Mitch's face. They both looked at David, who leaned against the counter.

"What? I'm crashing here for the night. I sucked back one

more than I should have. Either of you have a problem with that?"

Neither Mitch nor Jake said anything.

Finally, David pushed from the counter. "Okay, okay, I can take a hint." He loped from the kitchen and up the stairs, leaving the two of them alone.

Mitch leaned back. "I, um, take it you have something more to say on the Liz front?"

Jake nodded soberly. "Yeah, that I do."

Goliath stretched and yawned at his feet, reminding Mitch that he hadn't gotten much sleep in the past week himself. "So...?"

"So, I'm worried about you, that's all." Jake shifted awkwardly. "Look, I always liked Liz, Mitch. And despite what I said earlier... Well, I can't help thinking she had her reasons for, you know, doing what she did." He cleared his throat. "It might be a good idea for you to find out those reasons."

Mitch stared at his brother. He'd really never had a heart-to-heart with Jake, not even when Jake had agreed to be Mitch's best man seven years ago. Now he realized that it was because Jake didn't quite know how to put thoughts with an emotional twist into words.

"Aw, hell, you know what I mean."

Connor lay on the horn outside. A moment later, Pops yelled at him from an upstairs window to keep the racket down.

Jake pushed from the table. "The more things change, the more they stay the same, huh?"

Mitch wondered if he was referring to the exchange outside, or Liz. Either way, he would be right. "Yeah. I guess they do."

Something landed squarely in the middle of the table. Mitch stared at it, then at his brother, incredulous.

Jake rubbed the back of his neck looking as uncomfortable as hell. "'Night."

Mitch was shocked beyond speech as his gaze flicked from his brother's retreating back to the item he'd left behind.

As the truck tires outside crunched the gravel drive, he slowly reached out, turning the package over and then over again. A box of condoms. And not just any condoms, either. Latex, he'd suspected. But ribbed? Multi-colored? Flavored?

He burst out laughing, wondering what his brother would think if he knew the gift had come a couple of hours too late.

7

LIZ TOSSED her new handbag into the front seat of her Lexus then climbed behind the wheel. She was way too early. The sun was little more than a promising smear across the eastern sky. But she hadn't gotten much sleep last night, and if she sat around the house one minute longer, she'd go nuts. She'd rather wait at the McCoy place than here if Mitch wasn't ready yet.

Mitch...

She floored the gas pedal and tore out of the drive, nearly forcing an old pickup off the road. She waved her apologies to the driver and continued on through the cloud of dust her tires had kicked up.

What was it Mitch had said last night after...well, afterward? That their finally coming together had been worth waiting seven years for? Or something along those lines anyway. She tucked her hair behind her ear, then straightened the collar of her uniform. The words had haunted her all night. Despite his running from her that day at Gran's house, she suspected he'd planned on getting her between the sheets since the moment she arrived back into town. Well, okay, there hadn't exactly been any sheets.

Anyway, she couldn't quite shake the feeling that for him their...experience...had meant little more than to satisfy his curiosity. And that didn't sit well with her, which in turn caused her to be all the more upset with herself. After all, she wasn't exactly a despoiled virgin who now expected unwavering devotion from the man on whom she had bestowed her gift of chastity. She was a single female who'd had her share of consensual, intimate relationships with the opposite sex. Okay, she'd had all of two sexual relationships. Still, she had never felt this burning need to know exactly how the man felt about her after they'd...been together.

"I can't even *think* the words. Had sex. Made love. Did the nasty." She cringed at the last description, then forced herself to slow the speed of the car. At this rate, she'd end up passing the McCoy place.

Her agitation with herself and the world at large continued for the entire five-mile ride to his family's house. She tried to concentrate on the rolling landscape on either side of the road, to memorize the vivid green of the rows of corn and tobacco rushing toward maturity, to drink in the sweet smell of fresh earth and things growing, but all she could focus on was the further mess a single hour with Mitch had made of her life.

Finally the sprawling colonial farmhouse that Mitch had been raised in came into view. She immediately recognized some changes it had undergone since she'd last seen it. Where the exterior had been painted an austere white with black shutters before, it was now a heather gray, and the ornate cornices and remarkable lattice work shone a cardinal red. Her gaze swept up from the newly constructed front porch to the roof where the original smooth, tin sheeting shone. She squinted from where the just rising sun reflected off new curved windows with sunburst designs above each. Off to the right of the house a new red barn sat away from the old barn, which was little more than a haunted, gray monster.

She pulled into the drive, counting two cars and a truck in the drive. The truck was Mitch's. One of the cars likely belonged to his father. The other? Jake's?

She looked back up at the house, just then noticing that on the stretch of tin roofing over the porch sat Mitch in a pair of jeans and T-shirt. He was looking off toward the sunrise, seemingly unaware of her arrival. She moved her hand from the horn and instead got quietly out of the car.

She'd forgotten about his habit of climbing out of his bedroom window to sit on the roof. She slowly neared the porch, studying the serious lines of his face. He'd once told her he'd spend the entire night on the roof if he had a particularly tough problem to work out. Of course, back then his problems had come in the form of final exams and runaway pets.

She wondered what he worried about now. Was he, too, thinking about what had happened last night? Did he want to do it all over again? Her body hummed to life at the mere thought of being flesh-to-flesh with Mitch again. Or...

She caught her bottom lip between her teeth.

Or did he regret it?

Oh, this is ridiculous, she firmly told herself. Didn't she have enough to worry about? Did she really need to heap second-guessing his worries on top of all that?

"Liz? Lizzie Braden, is that you?"

David McCoy was stepping out onto the porch from the front door. At the sound of his brother's greeting, Mitch spotted her as well, his eyes smiling as he caught her gaze. She felt suddenly warm all over, then quickly stomped the reaction down.

"I heard you were back in town." David's gaze skimmed her figure in the waitress uniform. "I'd also heard you were as gorgeous as ever."

"Oh?" Mitch was talking about her. That was a good sign. Wasn't it?

David grinned. "Yeah, Jake filled us all in last night."

"Jake?" she said, unable to squelch her disappointment. "I didn't think he noticed things like that."

Within moments, Mitch had used a nearby tree and porch railing to lower himself to the ground, then came to stand next to her. "Me neither. Go figure, huh?"

Liz felt herself blush. She never blushed. Yet this was the second time she'd reacted in such a way since returning to Manchester. She fastened her gaze on David's face. He was her own age, and they'd shared a few summer catechism classes in younger years—that is when David could pull himself away from the girls and bothered to show up for them.

She smiled to herself. "So what have you been up to, David? Still hanging around the house, I see."

"Actually, I just stayed here for the night. I have a place in the city."

"Oh? Are you still in the army?"

"Nope. With DCPD now." He leaned against the porch column and crossed his legs at the ankles. The fairest one of the five brothers, he'd always had a way with girls, then women. In fact, Liz was probably the only one in the tri-county area who hadn't gone out with him.

He didn't miss her perusal and flashed one of his to-die-for grins. "Hey, I was thinking about coming back next weekend. If I do, you wanna catch a cup of coffee or something?"

Liz heard Mitch make a growling sound, then he stepped up to put his arm around her shoulders. The gesture made her feel...wanted...angry...confused. She shrugged his arm off and heard him say, "Sorry, little bro, but all Liz's cups of coffee are reserved for me."

"What is it with men and the issue of ownership?" She stepped from touching distance. "If I'm still around, I'd love to, David. We can do tea."

Mitch waved to his brother in mock dismissal. "Why don't

you and your hormones go back inside? Liz and I have to be getting to the diner anyway."

"You be sure to let me know if you guys need any help, you hear?"

Liz smiled at him. "We'll do that, David."

Mitch crossed his arms and stared at her through narrowed lids. Liz's uncertainties returned tenfold.

She knew that the male posturing that had just gone on meant little. The McCoys were legendary for their public skirmishes. If there wasn't an honest-to-God conflict to engage them in combat, they'd been known to make one up. In fact, she'd once watched Connor chase David up a tree just for looking at him wrong.

"So..." she said slowly. Why wasn't he saying anything? She didn't care what. He could at least make some inane comment on the weather. Something, anything, to stop her mind from reeling both from the nearness of him, and her fear that he regretted the night before.

"So," Mitch repeated.

Oh, that was just grand. Her gaze snagged on his mouth. That skillful, enticing mouth that had said and done so much yesterday, but was now quiet and unmoving. She cleared her throat. "Well, I guess we'd better get going. You know, to the diner."

"Yes, I guess we'd better."

She led the way, acutely aware that she walked in front of him and that he was probably watching her. A glance verified that his gaze was glued to her backside. She quickly got into the car and he did the same on the passenger's side.

They were halfway to the diner before either of them said anything.

"I wanted to talk to you about last night," she said.

"The consulting business must be good to afford this baby," Mitch said.

They stopped, looked at each other, then laughed.

"Go ahead," Mitch said.

"No, you first. I...I really didn't have anything to say, anyway." *Liar.* What was it with her? Lord knew she was the first to voice her opinion on anything. If she had a question, she asked it. And boy, was this question a doozy. Then why was she doing the mental equivalent of tucking her tail between her legs and making a run for it?

Mitch's wide grin told her he wasn't completely oblivious to her dilemma. And, damn him, he didn't appear ready to help her out of it either. She watched him stretch, then drape his arm across the back of her seat. "I was just saying that the consulting business must be good. You know. Your car and all."

She glanced around the rich interior without registering a thing. "Oh. Yeah. It's been very good." She relaxed slightly. Okay, maybe they were getting somewhere. "Ah, you've finally decided to share that you've been checking up on me, have you?"

He shrugged, the muscles beneath his T-shirt bunching then relaxing. She slowly drew the tip of her tongue across her parched lips.

He watched the movement, then turned to stare out the passenger window. "I figured it couldn't hurt, seeing as I'm getting nowhere fast in my investigation."

"I rate an entire investigation, do I?" She was acutely aware of his arm resting on the back of her seat. She tussled with the desire to lean her head back to entice contact.

"Uh-huh. Only problem is, I haven't been able to get answers to some very important questions."

"Such as?"

"Such as, Did you marry the damn guy or not, Liz?"

DAMN, but he wanted to touch her again. Anywhere. Everywhere. He'd been aware that finally having sex with her might offer up as many problems as solutions. What he hadn't counted on was wanting her even more now than he had before. Now that he knew exactly what making love to Liz was like, he had a helluva time thinking about anything else, including this damn investigation.

And her provocative, closed mouth wasn't helping matters any either.

"So?" he prompted.

"So what?"

He pulled his arm back from her seat, away from temptation. "Come on, Liz, did you run out on the guy before or after the 'I do's' were exchanged?"

He didn't trust the way she kept her gaze trained on the road, or the way her lips tilted up slightly at the corners. "Explain to me why it matters, and maybe I'll tell you."

He felt the sudden urge to punch her expensive dashboard. "Call me old-fashioned, but I don't make a habit of sleeping with somebody else's wife."

She finally glanced his way, but she'd lost the look of wariness she'd worn when she'd pulled up in front of his house. In its place was playful amusement. "Well, then, you should have thought about that before, don't you think?"

Mitch ground his back teeth together. Forget hitting the dash. He'd rather wrap his fingers around Liz's pretty little neck until something that resembled the truth came out of that wicked mouth of hers.

"We're here," she announced lightly, pulling behind the diner and parking between a Dumpster and the building.

He looked around the deserted alleyway, then grasped her wrist before she could get out of the car.

"Why didn't you park out front, Liz?"

She blinked several times in what could have passed for innocent confusion. Only he knew she was a long way from innocent and she was never confused. "You don't have to make a federal case out of it, ex-Agent McCoy. I just thought I'd leave the spaces out front for the customers."

She laughed and he released her. Spaces for the customers, his ass. Why did he have the sneaking suspicion he was being led on a wild-goose chase?

And why did he feel like wanting to do a little leading of his own?

8

TWO DAYS LATER, Liz hoisted the money tray out of the cash register, probing for the roll of quarters she was sure she'd seen somewhere in the drawer that morning. She smiled at the short line of people waiting to pay their lunch bills, then grabbed an extra roll of dimes instead, filling her palm with change before handing it to Charles Obernauer, the general store owner.

"Sorry, Charlie, I'm all out of quarters."

He jangled the small pile of dimes in his hand. "I'll have one of my boys run you over a couple of rolls when I get back to the store."

"Thanks. You really do have a heart, despite what everybody says about you."

He chuckled and ambled toward the door. Liz quickly took care of the other two patrons before grabbing the broom to sweep up the potato chips someone had dumped on the floor earlier and everyone else had tracked throughout the diner.

"Order up!" Mitch called.

Liz stared at him through the window that opened into the kitchen. He winked at her, then turned back to the grill, which was about the extent of their interaction since temporarily taking over the running of the diner two days earlier.

How was it that she felt so drained and he looked like he had just awakened from twelve straight hours of restful sleep in a big, soft, decadent bed? Especially since he'd been there since six that morning, the same as she had. And aside from burning a couple of pancakes early on, he'd slid into his old occasional role as short-order cook like a pro.

She remembered their last conversation, or at least what passed for a conversation, and wondered if not telling him she was as single as the day she was born had been a good idea. She knew it was only a matter of time before he found out that she and Rich had never even made it to the justice of the peace on the Beschloss lawn, much less gotten anywhere near saying the words *I do.* Ever since, Mitch had flirted and teased but kept his distance. He refused her offers to give him a lift into town. He gave her a casual wave at day's end. Nowhere was there any mention of the...incident...on that very table over there three days ago, much less any sign that they would be repeating the experience anytime soon.

She'd realized she'd left out an important option when she'd considered his possible reactions to their coming together: his ignoring the experience completely.

Liz bumped into Sharon, who had grudgingly agreed to come in on her day off to help. The young woman juggled the two plates she held.

"Sorry," Liz murmured.

"No problem," Sharon muttered back.

Liz made short work of the sweeping, then put the broom up and reached for the order Mitch was placing on the ledge. He opened his mouth.

"Don't you dare say it," she warned.

He leaned a tanned forearm against the window ledge, his ever-present T-shirt revealing a healthy length of toned biceps. "Say what?"

She snatched her gaze away from his tempting flesh. "You know what. Bo never yells 'order up.' He never has to, because we can see when someone's food is ready." She put the plate back on the ledge, forcing his arm off. "You forgot the cherub."

He stabbed the top of the Heavenly Hamburger bun with a chubby candy cherub and eyed, a little too openly, the way she straightened the skirt of her uniform. "Now, angel, you're never going to make enough tips to get out of this town if you don't adjust that attitude of yours."

"Good thing I don't need the tips then, huh?" she flung back, satisfied by the narrowing of his eyes.

"My, my, we got up on the wrong side of the bed this morning, didn't we?"

Liz tucked a stray strand of hair back up into her ponytail. The image of Mitch together with her bed made her hot all over. "And just what would you know about my bed, McCoy?"

Liz's feet ached, she was sure she would never regain full movement of her stiff neck, and she was positive she never wanted to see another rack of Paradise Pineapple Ribs, another Garden of Eden Pizza or Heavenly Hamburger again. She knew her ill humor wasn't just about Myra being gone until Lord knew when, or about every person in Manchester stopping in to check on Bo's status and having a meal while they were at it. Both of those things she could handle, for Bo's sake. It was Mitch and his constant flirting, his enjoying himself at her expense, that frayed her nerves and made her remember at the most inopportune times how intoxicating his kiss was...how intimately he had touched her...how wonderful he had felt between her thighs...and how much she secretly yearned for a repeat performance.

She put the plate of pizza down in front of the owner of the gas station.

"Ezra, do you order the same thing every day?" she asked the amazingly clean man with the sloppy eating habits.

"Yep. Look—" he fingered a slice of pepperoni with the

tip of his finger "—it covers all the food groups. Everything a growing boy needs."

She tallied up his order and put the white slip of paper next to his untouched napkin. "I hate to be the one to tell you this, Ezra, but I think you stopped growing twenty years ago." She smiled at the five-foot-six man with his graying hair and unusually proportioned face.

"Aw, Lizzie, and here I was about to update you on where things stand with the bet."

Liz's hands paused as she stuffed her order pad into her uniform pocket. In the busyness of the past few days, she'd completely forgotten that stupid wager she'd gotten herself into. She glanced at the man who had started it all and found him stacking two more plates on the ledge and calling 'order up!' with much relish.

"What do you mean, update me?" she said, stepping to the neighboring table and collecting empty plates. "I should think things are pretty much the same, aren't they?" She hiked a stack of dishes onto her hip. "Unless, of course, I stand to make more money than I did."

Ezra took a monstrous bite of pizza and grinned. "I'd like to tell you that was the case, Lizzie, I really would."

"But?"

"But...the odds have evened out. At this point, from what my figuring tells me, you and Mitch are running neck and neck."

Liz nearly dropped the plates to the floor. Neck and neck? Whatever happened to the favorable odds she had enjoyed only a few days earlier? The only odds that made any sense because no matter how preoccupied she was with the physical side of her relationship with Mitch, that's where she intended to keep things with him: physical. And very secret. That is, if she ever found herself alone with him again.

Why would she want a man to complicate things? Her life

was an out-and-out mess already. The career she'd worked so hard to build for herself didn't exist. Besides, she'd just left one man. She'd be nuts to switch her sights to another. Given her own allergic reaction to anything resembling an altar, she was coming to see that the whole marriage thing just wasn't in the cards for her.

"What?" she said.

"That's right." To her surprise, Ezra used the napkin instead of his purple-and-gold work shirt to wipe his hands. "Rumor has it you two were in the diner together alone the other night setting off fireworks of your own. Can't tell you how many people put their money on Mitch after that." His upper lip curled into what passed for a smile. "Good thing for me, too, 'cause I was coming out on the losing end of this bet if I had to cover all the wagers on you the first day."

Liz stood stock-still. Someone had spotted her and Mitch in the diner? Just exactly how much was seen? Her cheeks blazed.

"Guess that blush of yours says the rumor's true," Ezra crooned. "Want to join me for some of this pizza and tell me about it?"

Liz eyed the stringy anchovies snaking over the top of the pie and her stomach turned. She quickly squashed the temptation to pump the gas station owner for more information on what exactly the rumor going around town was. She recalled a similar such situation seven years before. An innocent food fight with Mitch over who would get the last bite of a shared bowl of ice cream had been made out to be something very carnal indeed by the time that rumor had made its way back to her. Liz rubbed her forehead with her free hand. Of course, not even that incident could equal what had happened there the other night.

"Sorry, Ez, but Eden pizza doesn't particularly appeal to me right now." She grabbed the empty cups on the table she was clearing and moved toward the kitchen. In fact, the only thing that appealed to her at that moment was exacting revenge against the man responsible for this whole mess.

She swung the door inward and crossed the kitchen to the sink where she unloaded the contents in her arms.

"You didn't collect your orders," Mitch said from behind her.

She turned toward him. "Mitch McCoy, what do you have to do with this rumor floating around town?"

"Rumor?" He quirked a brow and flipped a burger.

She picked up a rag from the counter and wrung it in her hands. "Don't play cute with me. You know perfectly well what rumor."

"I hate to disappoint you, but I've been stuck in this kitchen for the past two days." His grin did funny things to her stomach and she twisted the rag tighter. "I haven't exactly had time to indulge in any gossip."

He glanced to the rope she'd made out of the rag. She forced herself to stop wringing it. "Yeah, well, maybe you haven't had time to indulge in any, but you sure as heck could have started it."

"Oh, I see. I think I understand what this is about. Someone saw us in here the other night, didn't they?" His gaze slammed into hers. "How much did they see?" He skimmed her warm cheeks. "Never mind. We both know how little it takes to get rumors rolling in this town."

Liz cleaned off the cutting board he had used to slice onions, her eyes tearing in response to the pungent vegetable. She swiped at them with the back of her hand. "*Rolling* is about the word for it, considering that's probably exactly what the gossips have been saying we've been doing with each other."

His amused chuckle drew her gaze to him. She scanned his solid torso and the way his faded jeans hugged his delectable rear end. A twanging yearning vibrated through her. Good thing he was busy slapping the cooked burgers into altogether different buns or else he'd have made her pay for her lingering attention.

She cleared her throat. "You know, Mitch, there's something I'm having a difficult time understanding." She spotted Sharon picking up an order on the other side of the window and quickly asked her to look after the two customers she had left. The attractive young woman sighed. "Okay, but I get half the tip."

Liz motioned her off and turned back to Mitch.

"Why aren't you upset by all this attention the two of us are getting?" She examined him thoroughly.

"Upset?" He scraped the greasy cooktop with a metal spatula. "Why would I be upset?"

"Well...." She stepped a little closer to him so they wouldn't be overheard by the lunch customers who preferred the counter. "I would think that after...when I left... Well, the rumor mill probably worked overtime for months."

She regarded the tightening of his fingers on the wooden spatula handle. But when he looked at her there was nothing but that damnable gleam in his green eyes. "So?"

"So...." she said slowly. "Why would you purposely court more gossip about yourself now, especially since you know I'm going to be leaving again soon?" And especially since the other night was seeming more and more an aberration. As far as she was concerned, there wasn't nearly enough rolling around being done to warrant any gossip.

His devilish grin sent shivers shooting everywhere. "We're not anywhere near an altar now, Liz."

She crossed her arms. "So this is all just your idea of having a little fun then, is it?"

"Hmmm, you could say that."

She took the net from her hair and shook the restrained tresses loose. She didn't miss the slight darkening of his eyes. Mitch McCoy wasn't nearly as unaffected by her as he pretended. His cool, teasing behavior might be a puzzle to her, but one thing remained plainly clear: he still wanted her. She only had to figure out what to do so she could give herself to him. Again. And again after that.

She eyed his mouth. She didn't think even Myra's definition of fun included what had happened between her and Mitch—and what she hoped would happen again. At least once before she left, she quickly added.

In fact, she had hoped last night would prove just the opportunity. She had just turned off the house's lights when she heard a vehicle come up the gravel drive. She was pretty sure it was Mitch. But by the time she went downstairs and unlocked the back door, his truck was long gone. Needless to say, she'd gotten far too little sleep after that. She still trembled whenever she thought of the sizzling manner in which he had responded to her, the restraint he had used in the beginning, and the shaken way she had felt when they'd broken away from each other.

"You know, Mitch, if I didn't know better, I'd think you were purposely avoiding being alone with me."

He eyed her. "We're alone now."

"Sure, with half of Manchester just on the other side of that window."

She popped a blueberry left over from breakfast into her mouth. "I'd never have pegged you as the type to make late-night visits then back out at the last minute."

She turned toward the sink, nearly losing her balance when he grasped her arm.

"Late-night visits?"

She stared at him, heat stealing up from the touch of his fingers against her cool skin.

"Yeah, late-night visits." She felt her breasts tighten, warmth pool in her belly. She was in a sorry state if such a simple touch almost did her in. "Don't even try to tell me you weren't the one who drove up my driveway, then chickened out last night. Because I'm not going to buy it."

His passionate curse surprised her. "As much as I'd like to repeat what happened the other night, Liz, I didn't go anywhere near your place last night. Until I get some answers, I don't intend to go within a mile of your place."

She searched his face. She'd never gotten a look at the vehicle in her driveway. She had automatically assumed it was Mitch. Obviously she had been mistaken.

She shrugged. "Guess I was wrong then. Maybe someone used the drive to turn around." She took off her apron and folded it once. "Anyway, I've got a few errands to run."

Mitch's movements slowed. "Errands?"

"Uh-huh."

"First you tell me some stranger's watching your house—"

"I said I thought I heard a car pull up."

"—and now you're just going to take off without explanation?"

She loved to see him all worked up like this. "Yep." Liz glanced at her watch. "The lunch rush is over, and there are only a few people left. You and Sharon should be able to take care of things until I get back. I want to run over and ready Ruth and Bo's house for their return from D.C. tomorrow. And...well, I have a couple other things I want to see to."

"What things?"

She planted her hands on the metal island separating them and leaned closer to him. "Nothing that would help your investigation, I assure you."

He followed her lead, their mouths mere inches apart

above the counter. "Frankly, at this point, everything you do would help my investigation."

She smiled, enjoying the surge of power that came with her present position. "Still having a hard time, Mitch?"

"You're damn right I am." His gaze raked her face. "Why don't you wait until tomorrow to see to these other things so I can help you out with them?"

Oh, but that was plum. Mitch was actually showing a little emotion, proving he wasn't as unaffected by her as he seemed. But it was not exactly the type of emotion she was aiming for. "Help me out? Why would I need you to help me out?"

"Come on, Liz, let me in on this, will you? All I know so far is that you drove into town in the middle of the night wearing a bloodstained wedding dress, you're running from someone—"

"—I needed to get away from someone," she corrected again.

"Same difference," he shrugged, clearly aggravated. "It doesn't matter that I haven't been able to dig up anything more than that you've left a perfectly profitable business behind, and you no longer have a residence in Boston. As circumstantial as it all is, it adds up to you being in trouble."

She smiled. "But I'm not *in* trouble, Mitch. Why won't you trust me on this?"

He eyed her. "It's not you I don't trust, it's your judgment. What are the odds that you could be underestimating your situation and you could be in some sort of danger?"

"About zero to nil," she said, liking this conversation and her control of it a little too much. She stared at the unbending line of his lips, tempted to kiss the tightness from them and make him grin that irresistible grin again. "Anyway, if you want to talk odds, Ezra told me we're running neck and neck in this bet you got me into."

Mitch scowled. "Forget the bet. Our conversation doesn't have anything to do with that."

She glanced down at her uniform, wishing she had time to change out of it. But she was going to have to hurry as it was if she hoped to get back to the diner in time for the dinner crowd. "Oh, but you're wrong. Everything between us has to do with that bet, Mitch. That's the way you made it."

She started to turn away, then changed her mind. This opportunity was just too good to pass up.

Leaning farther over the counter, she tasted his lips with a quick flick of her tongue. She'd fully intended to stop there. Give him a little something to keep him guessing. But at the hungry look in his eyes, she couldn't resist meeting his lips full on.

It had been a long two days. He tasted of iced tea and mint. And his mouth was hot, so hot. She hated that the food counter separated them. Hated still that just beyond the window all conversation had stopped.

Yet all she could concentrate on was the quickening of the blood through her veins. Mitch's hand where he had thrust it through her hair to pull her closer. The tightening of her breasts beneath the fabric of her uniform. And the sensual sliding of Mitch's tongue against hers.

When she finally did pull away, she found herself as much a victim of her little tease as Mitch. Lord help her, but she wanted to vault over the counter and prove to herself that the other night hadn't been a figment of her imagination.

"Um," she barely managed, quickly licking her lips, loving the taste of him there. "I'd better get going."

"Yeah. I think that's a good idea."

She turned on her heels, the heat swelling in her belly chasing her exhaustion away.

CURSING UNDER his breath, Mitch checked on the meat items he had estimated he would need for that evening's orders, then stepped to the window overlooking the area of the diner for the fifth time in as many minutes. No one was visible except for old Josiah on his chair in front of the general store. Where in the hell was Liz? She'd been gone more than two hours. But it was more than her prolonged absence and the reason behind it that bothered him: the stranger he had spotted in town a few days ago was sitting at the same booth he and Liz had taken advantage of on the Fourth of July.

Given the relative emptiness of the diner—it was four o'clock and the only ones in there aside from the stranger were the Darton brothers, talking over coffee—the stranger stuck out like the red pair of shoes Liz had had on with her wedding dress when she'd driven back into town.

The guy had come in a half hour after Liz left, and, immediately upon spotting him, Mitch had adjusted his guess of the man's age as nearer to sixty than the fifty he'd thought before. He had graying blond hair, slightly aristocratic features, and was dressed in a lightweight summer suit, the white shirt he wore underneath looking as if it had come right out of the package. Those observations combined with the knowledge that the car the man drove was a rental told him that the stranger was convinced that what he sought was in Manchester or he wouldn't keep popping up there. It also told him that the stranger was very likely Liz's late-night visitor.

He watched Sharon serve him what had to be his third piece of cherry pie, the stranger obviously trying to involve her in conversation. The young waitress turned away from the table and Mitch called, "order up." Sharon stared at him, puzzled, but came to the window anyway.

"I don't have any orders," she said, ignoring his gesture to keep her voice down.

The stranger appeared not to hear her, his attention instead on the street outside, leaving the fresh pie untouched.

"Do you recognize that man?" Mitch asked.

"Which man? Oh, you're talking about my last customer. No. Never seen him before."

Mitch grimaced, realizing he wasn't talking to one of Manchester's most observant people. "What did he say to you?"

Sharon shrugged, evidently beat by the long hours she'd been putting in along with him and Liz. "Not much. Just asked if I knew somebody named Betsy something-or-other."

The stranger looked their way and Mitch handed Sharon a whole pie for appearances' sake. "Do you? Know anybody by the name of Betsy, I mean?" Mitch asked.

"Nope." Sharon sighed and reluctantly took the pie.

"Do you remember the last name?"

The waitress frowned. "I'm not very good with names. When he said Betsy, I already knew that I didn't know anybody with that first name, so I didn't pay much attention to the last. Why?"

Mitch watched the stranger reach into his pocket and deposit a couple of bills on top of his check and rise from the table. Trust Sharon to get curious now.

"Never mind. I just noticed he's new to the area and wondered if he needed any help."

Sharon sighed. "You want me to ask him?"

Mitch shook his head. He didn't want Sharon to strain herself. "No. Anyway, he just left."

The young woman looked relieved that she had one fewer customer to worry about and turned a beseeching look on him. "Can I leave now? I've already missed my favorite soap, my feet are so swollen there's not a chance they'll fit into the shoes I want to wear on my date tonight, never mind that I won't be able to put those new decals I bought for my fingernails on in time—''

Mitch stopped her with a wave of a hand. He glanced at the clock on the wall, then back at the tired Sharon. "Sure, go ahead. But would you mind coming in again tomorrow morning?"

"Do I have to? What with Ruth coming back and all..."

"I'd really appreciate it if you could," he said.

"Okay," she said grudgingly, pulling her purse out from inside a closed cabinet. "I'll see you then."

Mitch turned from the window and headed for the kitchen door. By the time he left the kitchen, Sharon was long gone, and the two Darton brothers were in need of refills. Trading jibes with them, he saw to their needs, then crossed to the table where the stranger had been sitting. He picked up the order and the money, then slid into the booth, watching the late-model Chevy pull from the curb across the street. The man had left a five-dollar tip.

Reminding himself to pass it on to Sharon in the morning, he stuffed the bill into his pocket and kept the remainder for the cash register.

Just sitting at the table again after what had happened on the fourth did strange things to him. He ran his hand over the smooth, clean surface, practically seeing Liz stretched across it in all her naked glory. He instantly grew hard. A brief look told him the thick folds of his full-front apron hid the proof of just how much he still wanted Liz.

Staying away from her for the past two days had been a virtual hell for him. Watching her move around in that tight little uniform. Catching the longing in her own eyes when she looked at him. Listening to the sassy little remarks he was sure were designed to get a rise out of him—and oh boy, did they—every time she came into the kitchen. All combined to leave him a shaking pile of lust when he finally got home. And he'd learned the hard way that cold showers were powerless against his growing need of her.

He tunneled his hands through his hair. But until he got some answers, the last thing he needed to do was sleep with Liz again. What if she *was* married to another man? What if the blood on her dress belonged to that man, and even now his decaying body was floating to the surface of the Boston Harbor? What if the guy just in here was a police detective come to question Liz about her husband's disappearance?

He let loose a series of mismatched curses. And what if he was the biggest fool alive because of his inability to read her? Problem was, he'd once thought he knew her better than anybody else. Then she had run out, telling him he had never really known her at all.

The flash of afternoon sunlight reflected off an approaching vehicle. He turned to stare at an old, battered...was that a Pacer? He hadn't seen one of those since the mid-eighties. The large, rounded car parked at the curb, and he noticed the temporary tag in the back window, right above where the bumper hung from two wires.

Liz got out of the driver's side.

Mitch rose from the booth so quickly, he nearly knocked the table from its anchor.

"What in the hell?" he muttered, hurrying to the door. Only Liz didn't head for the diner. Instead, she took that cursed wedding dress from the back of the car and crossed the street, walking in the direction of Peter's combination dry cleaners/men's wear/custom-tailoring shop. Glancing to where the Darton brothers stared at him from the counter, he offered up a half-assed grin, then turned to scowl out the front door. Changing his mind, he stepped to the counter and pulled the Dartons' freshly filled cups away from them.

"Sorry, guys, but the diner's closing for a half hour so I can get ready for the dinner rush," he said, keeping an eye on the cleaners across the street.

Moses Darton balked and reached for his cup. "Ruth never closes the diner."

"Yeah, well, Ruth's not here right now, is she? She's in D.C. looking after Bo." He grinned and stashed the cups under the counter. "Right now, I'm in charge, so blame me if you must, but I need you out. Now."

He budged the two from their stools and ushered them toward the door, not in a placating mood as he spotted Liz leaving the cleaners and heading in the diner's direction.

"Hey, there's Lizzie," Moses pointed out. "Bet she'll let us stay."

"Bet she won't, because neither one of you are going to ask her." Mitch patted them heartily on the back. "That is if you want me to let you run up your tab until your next paycheck from the mill."

Moses stopped short. "You're not saying you're going to cut us off, are you, McCoy?"

"This may come as a surprise, Moses, my man, but in a word, *yes.*" He opened the door for them.

Moses looked at his brother. "Did that sound like a threat to you?"

His brother led the way down the sidewalk, dragging his feet. "Yep, sure did sound like a threat to me...."

He watched them hesitate as Liz passed, but neither of them said anything more than hello to her. Mitch held open the door so she could enter, then hung the closed sign and turned the lock.

Liz blinked at him. "Why did you do that?" She glanced around the empty diner. "And where is everybody?"

Mitch advanced on her. "I told Sharon she could go home because she was dead on her feet. The others...well, I kicked them out."

A flicker of amusement colored her hazel eyes. "Why did you do that? The Dartons always stick around until din—"

"Enough of me answering your questions," he cut her off, glancing to her hand holding the key to what he guessed was the Pacer. "I think it's time you started answering mine."

The sides of her provocative mouth turned up into a sexy little grin. "Such as?"

He scowled at the way she eyed him suggestively, then grasped her arm, finding her skin sun-warm and much too silky. "Uh-uh, not here. Let's go into the kitchen. I don't want to be accused of setting you up again."

He lightly kicked open the swinging door and dragged her inside. He turned to find her smiling.

"It really doesn't matter much where we talk, Mitch. That closed sign you just hung will be enough for everybody. In fact, it's probably even better, given what the town already thinks."

Mitch fumed at her breezy attitude. "To hell with what the town thinks. I want to know what you're doing driving that clunker parked on the street."

She hiked a feathery brow. "Clunker? That's my new car."

"New ca..." He let loose a string of curses and restrained himself from giving her a good shake. "What did you do with the Lexus?"

She smiled coyly. "I got rid of it."

"You...got...rid of it," he repeatedly slowly, thinking her words made no more sense than she did. The expression on her face was that of innocent amusement. Too innocent. "Why would you do that?"

She shrugged. "It was more trouble than it was worth." She tucked a glossy strand of hair behind a tiny ear. "Besides, I always wanted a Pacer. They're so unique."

He narrowed his eyes. "You wanted a Pacer over a Lexus," he deliberated aloud.

An insistent knock sounded at the front door. Liz stepped to the window.

"It's Myra," she said. "She must be back from vacation. I'd better go let her in."

Mitch curved his fingers around her arm a second time, infuriated by the way she was stringing him along—and wondering just how long that string was. "I don't think that's such a great idea."

She stared up at him in raw need.

Every last thought threatened to fly straight from his head as he eyed the way she ran that sweet tongue of hers across her lips.

Then it struck him that she knew exactly what she was doing. Just as she had turned the tables on him emotionally two days ago, she had found another way to torture him and was doing a class-A job of it as well. He admired her lush little mouth, and wished he didn't want to reclaim it.

Liz glanced back through the window. "Mitch?"

"What?"

"I thought you might like to know that the Darton brothers are not going to leave now that Myra's back. They're all sitting on the edge of the planter outside waiting."

"Then let them wait," he ground out. He blamed his lack of diplomacy on the long day, on her tempting, frequent forays into the kitchen in her tight uniform, and on the growing list of unexplained, suspicious things she had done. What could possibly be next? A smoking gun?

He tightened his grip on her arm. "Now tell me...who's Betsy? And don't even think about telling me you don't know, because I know your pretty little behind is in trouble."

All trace of teasing drained from her face.

_____ **9** _____

MITCH RELEASED HER, confident he had earned her full attention. Confident, too, that if he kept touching her, he wouldn't
be able to stop.

"Betsy?" she repeated dully.

"Uh-huh. Betsy." He crossed his arms. "You want to explain who she is? Or could it be that I'm looking at her right
now?"

Another knock sounded at the front door, but Liz didn't
budge. In fact, she appeared not to have heard it at all. Mitch
rounded her and spotted the Darton brothers flanking Myra,
all three standing with their hands cupped over their eyes
against the glass, trying to see inside the diner. Mitch turned
back to Liz.

"Remember that stranger I told you about? The one I saw
in town the other day, and at the fairgrounds?"

He wished he knew what was spinning through that beautiful head of hers.

"Well, he stopped by the diner right after you left earlier.
Ordered three pieces of cherry pie, but only ate two. He
seemed to be looking for someone."

"Did you talk to him?"

"No. I was stuck back here in the kitchen. But he did ask
Sharon a few questions. One of them was if she knew a
woman in town named Betsy. Now, normally that wouldn't
get my attention. After all, I don't know any Betsy." He tilted
his head. "Or do I?"

She gave him a small smile then picked up a tray of refilled sugar containers. "I can't say as I know what you're talking about."

"Can't?" he murmured, gently forcing her to face him again. "Or won't?"

She stared at his chest and he found her sudden interest in his anatomy frustrating...and all too provocative.

"Come on, Liz. We both know Betsy and Liz are nicknames for Elizabeth. I'm not going to let you wriggle out of an explanation for this one."

She caught her plump bottom lip between her teeth. He repressed the urge to suck the pink stretch of flesh into his own mouth, then run his tongue along the smooth line of her teeth.

"What did he look like, this guy?" she asked, her gaze still riveted to his chest.

"What does it matter?"

She finally lifted her gaze to his. If he didn't know better, he would have sworn he felt her shiver. But whether it was because of the stranger they were talking about, or the need she must have glimpsed on his face, he couldn't be sure. "Just tell me, Mitch, what did he look like?"

"Put it this way, he didn't look like your type." Then again, what did he know about her type? He had fooled himself into believing *he* was her type long ago. "He was somewhere in his mid- to late-fifties, graying blond hair, nice suit."

He might have been way off about her shivering, but he was sure her muscles relaxed under his fingers. The sensation was backed up with a dazzling smile from her that nearly made him stumble backward.

"Like I said, I don't have a clue what you're talking about," she said, suddenly all sass and light. She glanced pointedly at his hands, then dragged her gaze up his arms, over his chest, then up to his eyes, making *him* shiver. Mitch could have sworn she had touched him, but her hands were calmly at her sides. If only he didn't want her to touch him. All over. Now.

His jaw tensed. "Liz—"

A series of knocks sounded again at the door, this time unceasingly impatient. He thought of all the questions he needed answered, all the little mysteries that followed in Elizabeth Braden's wake, and was filled with the desire to tie her up until she answered and solved every one. Let every person in Manchester knock at the door and wonder what was going on inside, he didn't care. They couldn't do much about it, short of dragging Ruth back from D.C. early. He stretched a kink out of his tense neck. The image of the curvy, luscious woman before him with her wrists and feet bound with lengths of rope and at his complete and utter mercy elicited a response in him that was downright dangerous.

He silently cursed and slid his hands from her warm arms. "We're nowhere near done with this conversation, Liz," he said, unable to resist smoothing her collar, feeling the heat of her flesh just below the surface of the stiff material. "Like I said before, you may look one hundred percent angel, but both of us know there's more devil in you than is good for either of us."

WHAT SHE WOULDN'T GIVE for her cell phone right about now.

In the middle of her grandmother's living room, Liz sat back on her heels, admiring her handiwork. She'd never cleaned so much so often in her life. She tilted her head to the side and frowned. A smudge was still apparent on the surface of the wooden side table. She pumped another spray of furniture polish on it and rubbed it from sight. Sexual frustration sure made for a spotless house.

There was only one man who could alleviate her problem, and since two nights had passed without a trace of him, she might as well put the polishing supplies away and plot out the next item she wanted to clean, scrub or strip.

If only she could keep her mind off stripping a certain someone instead of something, she'd be fine.

She felt like a sex fiend. Never had she been so fixated on something, completely incapable of thinking of anything else. She got up and headed for the kitchen. She hadn't realized how obsessed she was until she caught herself tracing highly suggestive shapes in the dust on the buffet table. She pushed her hair from her forehead with the back of her hand and flicked on the kitchen light, smiling when the room filled with warm, glorious light. She'd never realized how important electricity was until she didn't have it. Kind of like sex. Well, at least after you've had the right kind. And, oh boy, had Mitch ever showed her what *that* was like.

She put the can of furniture polish away, dropped the rag into the garbage, then leaned against the counter. The mere pressure against her hips made her shiver. Maybe she should give some thought to investing in some…pleasuring tools. She laughed aloud. They were sex toys, pure and simple. And she wished she had one or two about now. If only she was anywhere near convinced they would do the trick.

After washing her hands, she lethargically thrust the back window open a little farther, hoping for a breeze to cool the thick night air. No such luck. Air didn't come any hotter or more humid. She glanced at the clock she'd reset on the wall—11:00 p.m. Was that all? At this rate she was going to end up jogging to Mitch's in her T-shirt and white socks, his father and visiting brothers be damned.

If she did have her cell phone, who would she call? Ruth in D.C.? Sheila? She filled a glass with cold water and sighed. Ruth was probably already tucked in at her hotel room. And

Sheila? She realized she didn't have a clue what her ex-assistant would be doing right now. Sleeping? No. She'd told her once that she was very much a night owl.

At any rate, both of them were doing something more than she was at this moment.

The sound of tires crunching against the gravel drive caught her attention.

Mitch?

Her heart skipped a beat. She'd be damned if she didn't get all wet just thinking about him coming here now.

Then she recalled the night before and how she had mistaken that late-night visitor for him.

Stepping to the wall, she killed the lights. She listened as the vehicle moved farther up the driveway. Was it the stranger Mitch had told her about? If so, who was he? A P.I. Rich had put on her tail? A lawyer? Or had Rich hired his own police officer to come all the way down here and have her arrested for assault?

She crossed her arms tightly, then rubbed her fingers along her neck. Then again, it could be Rich himself.

No.

He'd never show up himself in the flesh. He'd send one of his cronies to bring her back.

Not that she'd go, mind you—

The slamming of a car door told her she was going to find out who the person was soon enough.

Out of a sense of self-preservation, she stepped silently back into the shadows, watching the open window. A figure walked by. It was too dark to make out who it was. But as he walked by the window, she noted the guy—and she was sure it was a guy—had to top six feet.

She bit her bottom lip. She should have turned on the outside lights.

Oh, this is ridiculous, she thought. Mitch and all his ravings about her being in trouble. For a minute there, she'd actually thought herself in trouble.

Still, when she heard the turning of a key in the lock, she grabbed the broomstick before flipping on the lights.

The man stepped into the kitchen.

"Jesus, Mitch, you scared the hell out of me."

Standing with his booted feet planted firmly on the tile, he considered her standing practically one with the wall, the blunt end of the broomstick pointed at his midsection. "If I had been an intruder, do you really think that would have done any good?"

She looked at the broom, then him. "Hey, don't knock it. You've never seen what I can do with one of these."

His grin made her feel alive all over. "Yeah, I hear a splinter in the backside can be quite deadly." He crossed his arms. "Tell me, Liz, what are you so afraid of?"

She propped the broom against the wall. "Nothing." *Now*, she added silently.

"Wrong wording. What *were* you afraid of?"

She shrugged. "You tell me. It's eleven o'clock at night. I'm a woman alone in a big ol' house. And there's a stranger in my driveway." She gave him a coy little smile. "Wouldn't that be enough to scare anyone?" She tucked her hair behind her ear, realizing what a mess she was. Unbrushed, sans makeup, cleaning products smeared across the front of her T-shirt, her old white socks bagging around her ankles, she probably looked a sight.

Why was it then that Mitch was looking at her as if she was the sexiest thing he'd ever laid eyes on? And why did she suddenly feel that way?

She cleared her throat. "What are you doing out here this late, anyway? Make a habit of dropping in on women in the middle of the night and using their spare key to get in?"

"Only one woman in particular. And I'm here for the same

reason you felt compelled to arm yourself with a broom. I was concerned for your safety."

She shivered under the weight of his suggestive look. "So you're here to protect me," she said, her voice sounding foreign to her own ears—rusty and far too suggestive.

She wanted to tease him. Continue the game of cat and mouse they indulged in at the diner. But her body had something else entirely in mind. Her nipples hardened to aching peaks. Her belly filled with a heat so intense she thought for sure he must feel it across the room.

Oh, how she wanted him. She wanted to feel him in her arms. Between her thighs. In her. Above her. Around her. She longed to feel him in every way there was for a human being to feel another.

And judging by the dark expression on his face, he wanted the same.

Mitch had struggled since earlier that evening with his decision to come over here. But the later it got, the more agitated he became. Yes, he told himself, part of the reason he was there was due to his concern for her well-being. Until he found out who the stranger was, and what exactly he wanted, he didn't like the thought of Liz being alone.

But his body reminded him of what his more compelling motivation was.

He wanted Liz.

As if reading his mind, she crossed the room and threaded her fingers through his hair, her pupils so large they nearly eclipsed the color of her irises. "So protect me then, McCoy," she murmured.

He claimed her saucy mouth with savage intensity. Damn it, he didn't care if she *was* married. If she *had* done away with her husband and stashed him in a Dumpster somewhere. Neither of which he'd been able to prove or disprove. He'd give everything he was to be connected to her again.

Everything. To lose himself in the feel of her sleek flesh surrounding him....

He hauled her against him, feeling the sway of her breasts beneath her T-shirt. Reveling in the hunger so clearly evident in her kiss. Loving the feel of her hands running wildly over his body.

He moved his hands up the backs of her thighs, then slipped them up under her skirt. His thumbs found the thin elastic of her panties and he slid them underneath. God, she felt so good. So damn right. He swallowed her low moan and plunged his thumbs into the narrow valley between her cheeks. Her breath caught. He thrust his tongue deep into her mouth even as he gently parted her, finding her sopping wet.

Groaning, he moved his arm to the backs of her knees and swept her up against his chest.

"That way," she said on a raspy sigh, pointing toward the hall door.

He didn't need directions. He'd traveled this route at least a thousand times in his mind. He just wished it wasn't so damn far. It seemed forever passed before he laid her down on the canopy bed in her room upstairs. His breath came in ragged gasps. His body felt about to explode.

He quickly stripped himself, then her, then lay down next to her, reaching for the condom in his back jeans pocket.

Before he knew what hit him, she was taking the foil packet from his fingers, tearing it open with her teeth, and quickly sheathing him. He nearly lost it right then and there.

He'd wanted this, their second time, to be better than the first. He'd wanted to go slow. To taste the sweet pleasures that lay between her thighs. Show her he could please her without pleasing himself. But she wasn't having any of that. Already she was straddling him, her palms against his abdomen, her breasts swaying tantalizingly just beyond his reach.

Then he was exactly where he wanted to be. Deep inside her.

She rocked her hips forward once. Then again. He grabbed the sheet under him in his fists. It took every ounce of self-control he had to just lie there, let her find her rhythm.

Finally she did.

And Mitch moved with her.

Never, ever had he seen a more beautiful sight than Liz, sitting astride him. Her mouth shaped in a perfect oval as she fought to hold off her climax. He thrust deeply up into her, watched the bounce of her breasts, the glistening of sweat beginning to accumulate on the velvety skin between them.

It was then he knew that he couldn't bear for her to leave. He'd realized after their first time together at the diner that sex with Liz was not merely the satisfaction of a long-burning lust. When he joined his body with hers, he was, pure and simple, making love.

He swallowed hard, now fighting off his climax. He let go of the sheets and cupped her breasts in his palms, plucking at her distended nipples, his gaze drawn to where their bodies were joined together.

He clamped his jaws tightly together. *No, no. Not yet.*

He needed a plan. He needed to find a way to convince Liz to stay. To show her they could have more together than just mind-blowing sex.

But how—

Liz's movements quickened, then ceased altogether as she needfully ground herself against him.

Mitch slid his arms under her knees, then lifted her. He ignored her soft protests and held her there for a long, torturous moment. Then with an almost violent thrust of his hips, he plunged deeply inside her. Once. Twice. Again.

His entire body quaked as she cried out above him.

His climax seemed to go on and on. Spasm upon spasm gripping him from deep within as her sleek muscles convulsed around him.

Long moments later, she lay on top of him, spent and breathless. He reached to push her hair from her face, distantly surprised to find his hand shaking.

"Liz?"

She softly hummed her response.

"When Bo and Ruth return—when we have time to ourselves—I want you to spend the day with me at my place. I have...I have some things to show you."

She didn't say anything right away. He listened as her breathing slowly returned to normal. Then she said quietly, "okay."

He closed his eyes and pressed his mouth against her temple. God help him, but he didn't know what he was going to do if he couldn't convince her to stay.

10

FINALLY, the chaos of the past couple of days held all of the promise of a return to normalcy when Ruth swept into the diner the following afternoon. Liz looked up from cleaning the last of the tables from breakfast, as did Myra, who was restocking the pies in the counter displays. Mitch belted out a hearty hello from where he cleaned up the kitchen. The only two customers, the Darton brothers, turned on their stools, holding up their coffee cups in salute.

Liz stuffed her rag into her pocket and rushed to hug her. "You don't know how good it is to see you," she said, leaning back to take a look into Ruth's strained eyes. "Is Bo with you?"

"No, after the trip from D.C., I made him go home and lie down. After all those tests, and the fear the doctor put into him, he was pretty beat."

Liz touched Ruth's arm. "You said you and Bo weren't going to be back until later tonight."

Ruth glanced around the clean, nearly empty diner. "That's because I wasn't up to a welcoming committee with a truckload of questions. I'm going to have to deal with them soon enough."

Ruth hugged her again so tightly, she crowded the breath from her lungs. Tears pricked Liz's eyes. What had brought this on?

"I can't thank you enough for looking after the place while

we were away," Ruth murmured and Liz caught a whiff of the lilac powder she always wore.

"Hey, don't I get some of that?" Mitch chided, emerging from the kitchen, his white apron securely in place.

"Of course you do, you big lug." Ruth hugged him as well. Her eyes twinkled mischievously as she eyed him. "Though I have to wonder if you'd have been so generous with your time if our Lizzie wasn't back."

Our Lizzie. Shifting from foot to foot, Liz tried to avoid meeting Mitch's gaze, but couldn't.

"Any other time I would give you guff for that remark," Mitch said. "But just because you and Bo are back safe and sound and healthy, I'll go easy on you."

Ruth grimaced. "Safe and sound we are, but healthy is a little ways down the road. Speaking of which," she began, pushing her hands against his chest and angling him back toward the kitchen, "I think we three ladies are going to review the diner's menu right now. I know you don't mind looking after the cooking a little while longer until we're done."

"Review the menu?" Mitch repeated with a droll grin. "That wouldn't happen to be synonymous with gossiping, would it?"

"That's none of your business. Now go. And I don't want to catch you listening in, either, you hear?"

Mitch feigned a grimace.

Liz crossed her arms and indulged in one of her favorite pastimes: watching Mitch walk away. Myra stepped up beside her.

"He looks as good going as he does coming, doesn't he?" her friend murmured, crossing her arms.

Liz elbowed her, and glanced at Mitch just in time to find him looking back at her. She didn't miss the devilish tilt to his lips, nor the wink that told her that that wasn't the last she was going to see of either his front or back side. She shivered in anticipation.

Ruth glanced toward the two men at the counter. "Moses and David, you're going to have to see after yourselves for awhile, but we're right over here if you need anything."

"Yes, ma'am," they said in unison without turning around.

Liz slid into the nearest booth when Ruth gestured for her to do so. Myra slipped in next to her.

"What's this really about?" Liz asked as Ruth collected a plate of cookies from the counter and sat across from them.

The diner owner plucked one of the plastic menus from its perch next to the sugar container and opened it in front of her, pushing the plate of chocolate chip cookies in Liz's direction. "What I said it was. We're going to revamp the meals we serve here."

Liz shared a glance with Myra, then took her notepad out of her uniform pocket. She pushed the cookies toward Myra, who grimaced.

"First of all, anything that moos goes," Ruth muttered, tapping her index finger against the long list of meat dishes the diner offered.

Myra's gaze shifted from the cookies to Ruth. "Are you serious?"

"As a heart attack."

Liz carefully reached out and closed the menu. "Ruth, are you sure you want to do this? I mean, while adding healthier selections is a good idea, you don't want to eliminate the plates that draw the people in."

"You mean the artery-choking killers?"

Liz experienced a burst of sympathy. Ruth was serious about altering the menu. And she guessed the decision was strictly an emotional one, a way to vent her fear about what had happened to Bo without letting on that it had bothered her. Only Liz could see it bothered her too much.

"Ruth? You can't turn the diner into a health food place." She carefully worded her argument. "This is not some trendy district in New York here. Manchester is full of meat-and-potatoes people. They may order your pineapple ribs, and they may like them, but you have to remember it's the ribs that pack them in, not the pineapple."

Myra leaned back to stare at her. "You really are a business consultant, aren't you?"

Liz ignored her, transfixed by Ruth's pinched expression and obvious dilemma. "I've got a suggestion, if you want to hear me out."

Ruth pulled a napkin out of the nearby holder and made a show of dabbing at her makeup, though Liz knew exactly what she was doing—drying the tears that had seeped from her eyes. "I don't know. Depends on what it's going to cost me."

Liz smiled softly and caught Mitch peeking around the kitchen window. Her cheeks heated and she lowered her voice. "It's not going to cost you a cent. Even though in my last contract I got..." She quoted a figure.

Both Ruth and Myra stared at her in thinly veiled shock.

She laughed. "No joke. But, hey, I made the mistake of getting involved with the boss. That same boss froze my accounts when I broke our contract."

Myra gave in to temptation and broke off a piece of a cookie. "Froze your accounts? How could he do that?"

Liz noticed that the shine of curiosity had returned to Ruth's eyes and she relaxed slightly, deciding sharing a little of herself to help Ruth concentrate on something other than her own ordeal was worth it.

Still, it was a bit difficult to push the words past her throat. Especially since Mitch—despite Ruth's stern warning—was trying his level best to hear what was being said at the table across the room.

She stumbled back on subject. "How could he do that? Simple. He, um, my boss was the vice president of the bank where I had my personal and business accounts."

Ruth leaned her forearms on top of the closed menu. "This the guy you were going to marry?"

Liz nodded, relieved she had put it that way. After what had happened between her and Mitch seven years ago, Ruth could easily have said, "This the *other* guy you were going to marry?" But what had occurred between her and Richard Beschloss in no way, shape or form came close to what she had once felt for Mitch. What she still felt for him.

She swallowed and waited as Myra rose from the table and brought back three cups and a full pot of coffee.

The Darton brothers groaned about the loss of their coffee and Myra told them to put a sock in it.

The quirky brunette sat down again and sighed. "So that explains why you took your old job back here. You really do need the money."

Liz folded the top sheet of her notepad, purposely not mentioning the hefty money order she had mailed to Sheila that morning to cover her severance pay. She'd gotten more than she expected for her Lexus in the neighboring county and had sent half of it. Even with the mere pittance the Pacer had cost deducted from it, she had more than enough with which to move on. Funny thing was, she didn't feel in a hurry to go. "Guess I like to learn things the hard way."

Myra sat back in the booth. "Learn what? That all men are dogs?"

This time it was Liz's turn to stare. "Dogs?"

"We wouldn't happen to be talking about Harvey now, would we?" Ruth asked.

Liz glanced out the window, seeing old Josiah across the

way rocking in his chair. "I didn't hear the infamous Harley when you came in yesterday."

Myra twisted her lips. "Yes, I'm talking about Harvey, and no, you didn't hear the Harley because I rolled it into a ditch night before last somewhere outside Moody, Alabama."

A laugh exploded from Liz, earning a glare from her friend. "Sorry," she said, and tried to make herself look as if she was. "But I was just imagining Harvey's face when you did that."

Myra shrugged her slender shoulders. "Wish I could tell you. Truth is, I did it after he fell asleep at a motel, and left before he had a chance to find out what I'd done."

The three of them exchanged glances, then burst out laughing.

"What did the dog do?" Ruth asked. Liz eyed her, comforted to find little trace of her earlier worry visible.

Myra leaned closer. Liz noticed that Mitch very obviously stood in the kitchen window drying a large pot, and the Darton brothers had grown awfully quiet at the counter.

"*Dog* isn't exactly the word I'd use to describe him, Ruth. That wolf...coyote...dingo...well, as soon as we got down to Mobile—that's where my mother's family is from—he made this big production of having something to give me. Something, he said, that I'd been wanting for a long time." She paused and closed her eyes. "I swore he meant to ask me to marry him. I went out and bought a new dress, got all dolled up. Then over dinner at a crab place—" her eyes flicked open, revealing flames licking in the brown depths "—he gave me this...this box. You know what was in it? A dog collar."

Liz blinked at her. "Did a dog come along with it?"

"Yeah. Harvey." Myra rolled her eyes. "Of course a dog didn't come with it. It was a collar for humans. You know, a thick piece of black leather with silver spikes that you wear around your neck?" She half circled her own neck with her index finger and thumb. "This one had a tag attached. It said Harvey's Biker Chick."

Liz cringed and looked at Ruth, neither of them finding the information particularly shocking. Myra had a long history of choosing thoughtless guys. This was the first time, however, that Myra had dumped one of them, instead of waiting around and being dumbfounded when they deserted her.

"You're better off without him," Ruth said, giving her forearm a squeeze.

"That's what I thought." Myra sniffed.

Liz handed her a napkin, and Myra took a swipe at her arm. "Knock it off, Braden. Your luck with men isn't any better than mine."

Ruth raised a penciled brow. "She's got you there, Lizzie." She shot a reprimanding gaze at Mitch and the Dartons, who were openly watching them now. "If you guys don't want to lose your stool privileges, you'd best be about your business."

Mitch disappeared from sight and the brothers promptly turned back toward the counter and grabbed their empty coffee cups.

Liz laughed, loving that Mitch was curious as hell about what they were discussing.

"Speaking of Mitch..." Ruth trailed off, looking at her.

"Oh, were we? I didn't hear his name come up," Liz said, swearing sometimes the woman could read her mind like an open menu.

Ruth smiled knowingly. "I want to know what you two were doing in here alone together when I called on the fourth."

Myra pretended to be about ready to fall out of the booth. "What?"

"Oh, quit it, you two. His stopping by was completely innocent." Well, at least that much was true. They didn't have to know what happened after that. Or what had happened again last night....

"Uh-huh." Myra finished the cookie she was working on, and part of another, then pushed the dish toward Liz.

Ruth took one herself. "That's not what I heard. In fact, word is the odds on that bet is tipping over into Mitch's favor."

Liz stared at her.

"You guys *are* repeating history," Myra mumbled, clearly dismayed.

Ruth waved her hand dismissively. "Never mind her," she said to Liz. "She'd gone out with every available guy in the tri-county area by the time Mitch came back. The instant he rolled into town, she thought her prospects had improved."

Myra poured cream into her coffee. "Until Liz came back, too."

Liz stared at her friend. Why was she the last one to hear this? "You're interested in Mitch?"

Myra shrugged and stirred her coffee. "Not interested really. I guess *curious* is more the word. I always wondered what you two used to do together to look so...blastedly happy."

Ruth munched on a cookie and studied Liz's face. "They couldn't have been too happy or Liz would never have left."

Feeling as if she had revealed too much about herself already, Liz plucked a cookie from the small stack remaining. She began to put it back, then instead took a hearty bite. "Can we get back on topic, please?"

Ruth wiped crumbs from her hands and stared at the menu in front of her again. "Do you really have some ideas about changing the menu?" she asked.

Liz nodded, relief suffusing her tense muscles. Why was it whenever Mitch was brought into the conversation, she immediately found herself on the defensive? She stole a glance toward the kitchen, but he was nowhere in sight.

Myra slipped from the booth. "Don't look now, but the flocks descend."

Liz stared through the window overlooking the street. Charles Obernauer, along with a couple of his cronies, approached from one side, while Ezra headed another group closing in from the other. Liz popped the remainder of her cookie into her mouth, regretful she didn't have time to chase it down with some coffee.

Myra gathered the pot and the cups, but Ruth refused to give up the menu.

She glanced at Liz. "Guess we're going to have to wait until these guys' rumbling stomachs are filled before we can finish this conversation."

MITCH COOKED his way through the dinner rush. Ruth had attempted to take over, but he had chased her out of the kitchen to her usual job of tending the cash register and catching up on the books Liz had looked after the past couple of days.

He flipped four burgers, then peeked around to catch a glimpse of Liz waiting tables. The early-afternoon sun slanted in through the windows, setting her glorious blond hair aglow and bringing her lush figure into relief under her white uniform. He lowered his gaze to her nicely curved legs and the gentle sway of her hips. The woman could put a real angel to shame. What was amazing was that the beauty she radiated on the outside came from a very deep source within. Somehow, over the course of the past week and in the shadow of their private midnight meetings, he had forgotten that.

But while she had sat with Ruth and Myra discussing whatever it was that women talk about, his gaze had been drawn to her time and again, catching the warmth and compassion in her gestures, her smiles, the way she gave whoever she talked to her complete attention. What he would have given to be able to hear what they were talking about.

He caught a whiff of something burning. Biting back a curse, he rushed back to the grill. One of the burgers was a little darker than it should be, but, irritated, he slapped it on a bun anyway.

Now that Ruth was back, it was time to put his own plan into motion. One that would, he hoped, throw a permanent monkey wrench into her plans.

He slid the four ready plates onto the ledge. "Order up!" he bellowed.

Liz jerked to stare at him and he couldn't help grinning, until he got a gander at Ruth's questioning gaze. Clearing his throat, he turned back to his duties, keeping an eye out for Liz.

"Ruth's going to have a piece of your rear end for that one," she quipped, taking two of the four plates while Myra gathered the others. "And it's a shame really, seeing as it's nice just the way it is."

Mitch moved toward her, relieved six inches of wall and two counters separated them, because he wouldn't have been able to resist tasting her sassy lips otherwise. "Why is it, Liz, that you're all mouth when others are around, but you clam up when we're alone?"

The Darton brothers and Charles Obernauer chuckled from the counter. She glared at him, as if daring him to say something more. Like how she wasn't so quiet when they were alone after all, and, in fact, could get quite loud. But he kept the words, arming himself for the next time he could corner her.

Myra rolled her eyes and turned from them. "You two make me sick."

Liz squeezed out from behind the counter to deliver the orders.

Mitch didn't miss the amused expressions on the other men's faces as he made a point of watching her walk away. She wasn't the only one who could enjoy a great departure. The sexy sway of her hips, and the slight upward tilt to her chin, made her all the more attractive.

"Whew, things sure are getting hot in here," Moses Darton said, fanning himself with his paper napkin. "Ruth! You want to turn the air up a bit?"

Laughter rumbled through the diner and Liz nearly dropped the plates she'd cleared from an empty table. Mitch wiped his hands on a towel and had begun to turn away when the flash of the sun reflecting off the opening door stopped him. From the beige-and-white checked suit jacket up to the new arrival's graying blond hair, Mitch scanned the unwanted visitor.

Mitch crushed the towel in his fingers, his muscles tensed to the point of snapping as he stared at the man. He had no doubt that Liz's late-night visitor from two days ago was now seating himself at the booth she had just cleared.

Myra's head popped into the window. "You got Ezra's pizza ready yet?"

Mitch stared at her; her frizzy dark hair blocked his view of the stranger.

"It'll be out of the oven in a couple of minutes," he answered automatically, trying to look past her to where Liz poured the stranger a glass of water and appeared to take his order. The guy looked at her a little longer than necessary, but nothing in his demeanor spoke of surprise or curiosity.

That means he already knows who she is.

Mitch's stomach tightened and Myra drummed her midnight-blue fingernails on the ledge then turned away with a sigh.

But if he already knew who she was, then why didn't she recognize him?

The questions lined up one after another as Liz moved to the pie display and served—what else?—a piece of cherry pie.

He threw the towel to the preparation counter in front of him and started for the kitchen door to find out exactly who this man was and what he wanted with Liz. Halfway there, the oven timer buzzed, halting him in his tracks.

Not bothering to hide his irritation, he let loose a string of curses that would curdle the cream in the customers' coffee. He was forced to abandon his hasty plan...for now. But he would confront the guy the moment the lunch crowd let up.

Nearly burning his hands as he removed Ezra's pizza from the oven, he slid the food onto a serving plate and hurried back to the window, staring at the way Liz moved around the place as if not a thing was wrong.

Didn't she remember the stranger he'd told her about? Didn't she see the guy was staring at her right now? Judging by all her normal reactions he guessed no. Then again, he reasoned, she had been gone seven years. And even back then she hadn't come near knowing all the residents the way he had. He frowned. As she herself had said, everybody in Manchester was strange to her.

Urgently, he put the pizza on the ledge. Near the cash register, he spotted Liz taking off her apron, the stranger's gaze focused outside the window, then trailing to her.

"You didn't say 'order up,'" Myra complained, popping up in the window again.

"So sue me," he challenged without looking at her.

Liz was saying something to Ruth, then she laid her apron on the counter and strode toward the door. Myra picked up the plate, and Mitch grabbed her arm.

"Where's she going?" he asked.

"Who?" Myra stared at his hand. "Liz? She said she had something she wanted to pick up at the cleaners before they close for the afternoon."

Realizing he still had a grip on Myra, he quickly released her, his gaze plastered to the stranger watching Liz cross the street outside the diner. Adrenaline pumped through his veins.

If the guy was a cop, then Liz was going to hand him his first and most damning piece of evidence against her.

He began to untie his apron, then abandoned it, telling himself he didn't have enough time. As busy as it was at the diner, Liz didn't dare stay longer than a couple of minutes at the cleaners.

He pushed open the kitchen door and stalked directly to the stranger's table.

"You looking for somebody?" he grumbled.

Dragging his attention from the street and Liz, the stranger blinked up at him.

"Pardon me?"

Mitch met the man's stare. "I asked if you were looking for somebody."

"No." He gestured to his untouched food. "I just stopped in for a piece of Bo's famous cherry pie."

Mitch seethed. How good could the guy be if he didn't even do his research? "It's Ruth's," he pointed out.

"Okay," the stranger said slowly. "Then Ruth's famous pie. With two names on the diner, I had at least a fifty-fifty chance of getting it right, eh?"

Mitch reined in the desire to take the pie and make the guy swallow it in one bite so he could kick him out. But he couldn't, not without knowing if he was some sort of police detective from another city. Say, Boston?

Ruth hurried up to him. "Mitch, are you hassling my customers?"

He said nothing.

"No, ma'am, Mitch...isn't it? Mitch and I were just having a harmless conversation," the man said and flashed a cool smile.

Ruth hovered uncertainly, looking about ready to grab Mitch by the arm and yank him away from the booth.

"Actually, we were just about to take our conversation back to the kitchen, weren't we...Dick?" he added the name for good measure, drawing a surprised expression from the neatly dressed man seated in front of him.

Ruth sighed in exasperation. "Well, then, go on and do it. You're disrupting people's lunches out here."

Mitch swept his arms in the direction of the kitchen door. "After you."

Reluctantly, the man rose from his seat and started in the direction he indicated. Mitch flicked an uneasy gaze toward where Liz was just entering the dry cleaners.

"Have we met somewhere before?" the man asked.

The kitchen door swept closed behind them and Mitch grasped his nicely tailored lapels and carried him to the wall where he flattened him against it.

"I want to know who you are and what you're doing in Manchester," he ground out, hardly recognizing the dark tone of his voice. "Are you a cop?"

Beads of sweat broke out on the older man's forehead. "A cop? No, no. I thought you knew who I was when you called me Dick out there. I'm...I am a private dick...detective from Massachusetts. If you'll just let me go for a minute, I'll show you my card."

Mitch stared him down. All at once, everything came together, and what the man was saying made perfect sense. He should have known from the first. He'd always been so capable in his jobs as FBI agent and as P.I. But add Liz to the picture, and he missed even the most obvious of clues.

Reluctantly, he released his grip and smoothed down the wrinkled lapels. His hands shaking, the stranger rifled through the inside pockets of his jacket, finally pulling out a bi-fold identification that listed him as Don Secord, P.I.

Mitch eyed it long and hard. "You're not in Massachusetts anymore, Secord."

The stranger blinked at him. "No, I—"

"Who are you working for?" Mitch interrupted.

A peculiar clicking noise sounded as Secord swallowed. "I can't tell you that. That's privileged information."

"Well, I'm making it unprivileged." Mitch stepped ominously closer to him.

"I'm telling you I can't give you that data. But—but I can tell you who I'm after."

Mitch waited.

Secord rifled through his pockets again, this time coming out with a three-by-five photograph. Mitch snatched it from his fingers and turned it around. His throat tightened as he stared down at the dark-haired woman. *Liz.*

"Her name's Betsy Braden. Someone at the store across the street told me she worked here. I didn't recognize her at first, but I'm positive she's the blonde that just left the diner."

Mitch cringed. *Betsy Braden?* Whatever possessed Liz to take on such a pretentious name? He eyed the man before him, noting his expensive clothes and his smooth demeanor. Given his own experience in the field, this guy was no B-movie private dick. He was a professional. And professionals cost big money.

He stuffed the photo into his back jeans pocket, and, in the same move, slid out his own identification. "Well, Don Secord, P.I., I'm Mitch McCoy, ex-FBI, now fellow P.I.," he said, laying on a heavy southern drawl. "And I don't much like northerners down this way bothering the residents of my town."

"FBI?" The man eyed his apron and the kitchen they stood in.

"Yeah, ex-FBI." Mitch grabbed his lapels again and swung him toward the door. "I'm going to give you two minutes to reach the county line. If you're not out of here by then, I'm going to have a few of my old buddies introduce you to a little cell up D.C. way."

The man reddened. "You can't hold me."

"Try me," Mitch challenged, wondering if Connor or David could help him out if push came to shove.

"On what charge?" Secord sputtered.

"Harassment for starters. Trespassing on private property if you make things difficult, and a whole host of other charges, including stalking, that will find you in the area longer than you planned, if you want to press the issue."

The dick shrugged and nodded. "I'm gone as soon as you let me go. In fact, I'll be out of here so fast you'll have to wonder if I was ever here."

Mitch tightened his fingers, wondering if Liz was still at the cleaners. To be on the safe side, he jostled the P.I. toward the back door.

"Go out the back way."

"What about my bill?"

Mitch scowled. "I'll get it."

He released the man, and, true to his word, he scrambled toward the door in two seconds flat, nothing left of him except the lingering smell of his expensive cologne.

Stuffing his ID back into his pocket, Mitch entered the main area of the diner just in time to see Liz coming through the front door, hanging the clean wedding dress up on the coatrack just as a flash of beige scrambled past the window. Moments later, the blue rental car squealed away in a streak of color.

He let out a long breath and hung his chin to his chest.

Thank God. Didn't Liz realize that no bloodstain could ever be completely cleaned from any material? That the chemical Luminol could illuminate the tiniest of traces? He dragged his fingers through his hair and glanced up to find everyone in the place staring at him.

Ruth faced him.

"Cough up your apron, McCoy. As of this moment, I'm officially retiring you."

Liz strode up to stand behind her.

He reluctantly reached to unfasten the ties behind his back. "Were the reports on my cooking that bad?"

Ruth looked ready to boil him fully clothed. "On the contrary. Your cooking gets raves. It's your manner with the customers that leaves something to be desired." She took the apron he offered. "First I hear you chased two of my best customers out of here yesterday afternoon then closed the joint. Now you're just plain chasing customers out. What's gotten into you?"

He nearly told her it wasn't *what* had gotten into him, but *who* had gotten into him. Namely Elizabeth, alias Betsy, a.k.a. Liz, Braden.

He watched Liz reach over to a nearby table and halt a bobbing cherub, trying to keep a straight face but failing miserably.

"Boy, the thanks I get," Mitch mumbled as he slanted a gaze toward the Darton brothers still seated at the counter. Moses Darton cleared his throat.

Mitch looked at Liz. "So are we on for tomorrow? Shall I pick you up at, say, eleven o'clock?"

"Tomorrow?" she repeated.

He nodded in Ruth's direction, hoping Liz hadn't forgotten last night when she'd said she'd spend the day with him as soon as they had a day to themselves. He had but one shot to convince her to stay. And, damn it, he was going to take it.

Liz's face flushed with color. "Oh. Yes. Yes, um, eleven's fine."

Mitch reached into his pocket and handed Ruth a five-dollar bill. "To cover the pie."

"Gee, thanks. Now go on. Get out of here."

He grinned at the quick way she took the offered money. "Do I still get to come back as a customer?"

Ruth smiled back. "The place wouldn't be the same without you."

11

THE FOLLOWING MORNING, Mitch lay on the horn, unsurprised by the lack of movement in Liz's house. Goliath, sprawled across the bench seat, whined. It was ten after eleven. If he had known Liz had no intention of making it on time, he could have checked a couple more items off the list of things to be done around the one-hundred-and-sixty-four-acre McCoy spread.

Where was she?

Switching off the engine, Mitch climbed from the truck, hesitating only slightly to allow a reanimated Goliath to jump out before closing the door. He strode toward the back of Liz's grandmother's house. Finding the key over the back window again, he then opened the screen door, and settled his hand over the tarnished door handle. It turned easily without the key.

"Damn it, Liz, you should know better."

He stepped into the mudroom and was nearly knocked over when Goliath barreled inside, sniffed around his feet, grabbed something then ran back outside. Banging his knee on a low-lying table, Mitch groaned and clutched his leg until the throbbing pain passed. He groped around, plucking a shoe from the floor. He stared at it. It was not just a shoe, but one of those maddening red shoes she'd been wearing the night she rode into town.

Holding the shoe, he carefully made his way into the kitchen. The room was dim, in spite of the hot sun outside.

He blinked, adjusting his eyesight, then settled his gaze on the window. He stepped over to it and opened the curtains that blocked even the dimmest ray.

He turned to find a cot set up in the far corner. He was almost sure it hadn't been there the night before last. Liz's slumbering outline was plainly visible under the tangled, thin cotton sheet, both it and a pillow pulled over her head. A bare foot and part of a shapely calf stuck out the end. He resisted the urge to run a finger over the delectable arch.

There would be time enough for that later.

"Liz?" he said, searching for signs of life.

Still holding the shoe, he reached over and closed his fingers over a corner of the sheet—a corner well away from her foot.

"Oh, Elizabeth?" he tried again, this time a little louder.

Not even a twitch to indicate she had heard him. Staring at the sheet he clutched in his fingers, he debated yanking it back. He shifted his gaze to the form underneath, trying to discern if she wore anything. The woman didn't lock her door, wasn't even alert to the fact that there was someone in her temporary bedroom/kitchen. It wouldn't surprise him in the least if she was sleeping in the buff.

He jerked his hand back empty. Oh no. He knew his limits. And a naked, sleepy Liz was a sight even he wouldn't be able to handle, plans or no.

"Betsy!" he yelled, crossing his arms.

She sprang up so quickly she startled *him*. He stepped back, well out of attack range, watching her toss the pillow to the floor. Her hazel eyes were wide and unfocused, her blond hair a captivating tangle around her sleep-creased face.

"Wh-wh-what?" she whispered, her gaze darting around the kitchen, then back to him.

She moaned and flopped back to the mattress. "Oh, it's you. For a minute there I thought you were..."

It would have been the perfect opportunity to pump her for information on exactly who that was. But the truth was, he couldn't have pushed anything past his tight throat if he tried.

Liz wasn't naked. But she *was* the next best thing.

He eyed the sheet bunched around her knees, his searing gaze dragging upward to where a triangular scrap of lace and satin barely covered the lush wedge of hair beneath. A brushfire swept through his groin. He forced his attention away from the naughty string bikini and up her toned, perfectly molded torso to where the cropped T-shirt barely stretched over the satiny swell of her breasts, the undersides clearly visible. He watched the movements of her chest as she lazily reached for the sheet.

"Mitch McCoy, have you no shame?"

"What?" he asked, quirking a brow and enjoying the rosy flush that crept up her lovely neck and across her cheeks. "I was just noticing that you've been doing some shopping." He swallowed hard. "Anyway, you don't have anything I haven't seen before."

Which was the truth. He had seen it all. He'd sampled the luscious wares, too. And he'd be damned if he didn't want to do it all over again. He shifted from foot to foot, trying to find a comfortable position where his jeans didn't hurt so much. If he didn't cool it, he'd end up between those toned thighs before she could blink her sleepy eyes. The arousing image made his jeans even tighter. He eyed the rickety cot, wondering if it would support both their weights....

"What are you doing sleeping in a cot in the kitchen, anyway?"

"It got a little too hot upstairs last night," Liz said, dangling her tanned legs over the side of the bed. "What are you doing holding my shoe?"

He stared at the red, strappy object in his hand. It took a moment to remember how it got there. He tossed it onto the bed next to her, resisting the temptation to ask her to put it and its partner on, just so he could see how she would look in her present attire...and the red shoes.

Briefly closing his eyes against the rage of emotion threatening to erupt, he dragged in a deep breath and counted backward from ten. By the time he opened his eyes again, she was standing, the sheet draped haphazardly around her waist.

"The thing nearly killed me when I came in the door," he said, watching her navel wink at him as she tucked in the sheet. "A door, by the way, that you left unlocked all night."

She pushed her jumble of shiny hair back from her face. "I did not. I woke up this morning for a potty break and I unlocked it then." She smiled up at him. "I figured I probably wouldn't hear your knocks because I'm a pretty heavy sleeper."

"I'll say."

He battled to keep his gaze above neck level, but didn't find the view there any less attractive than the rest of her. Liz had the type of face that inspired men to sculpt. He gazed into her wide eyes and altered the thought to paint. But it would take years of experimenting with different shades of blues, browns and greens to duplicate the remarkable color of her eyes.

He made a point of looking at the watch on his wrist.

"Well if you have any more potty breaks you'd like to take, I'd recommend taking them now." He'd known it would be a mistake to come in here this morning. That's why he'd sat for fifteen minutes in the truck, blowing the horn. "And put something on."

Her tempting little lips bowed into a smile. "Do you really want me to do it?"

"Yes. Now get a move on. Time's a-wasting." She started to walk toward the bathroom. "And you can wear anything but that shirt and those skimpy cut-offs. The whole point of this adventure is to spend some time together outside of bed, if that's all right with you."

She halted in the doorway, smiling at him. What was she up to now? He found out when she dropped the sheet to the floor and provocatively stepped from the puddle of material and away from him. He noticed then that the panties didn't have a back. The heat in his groin gushed through his limbs as he stared at the red satiny ribbon that came dangerously close to disappearing into the shallow crevice between her firmly rounded cheeks.

He closed his eyes, trying to remember what they called the downright indecent undergarment. But for the life of him, he couldn't concentrate on anything other than the image of her tight, lush rear end, her narrow waist, and the provocative way she had teased him.

The bathroom door slammed and he relaxed, if only a bit. He quickly strode one way in the cramped kitchen, then the other. The woman was bad enough when she *wasn't* trying to provoke a reaction.

The toe of his boot caught something. He stared down at what looked like a blue dart on the warped linoleum. He picked up the fine-pointed game piece and weighed it in his hand. What was Liz doing with a dart? Possibly throwing it at a picture of him? Slowly turning toward the opposite wall, he discovered the answer.

Far from the picture of himself he half expected, the wall was covered with the various brochures he'd seen her with over the past week. Brochures on cities as far away as Seattle, and as near as Richmond. Puzzled, he counted twenty of them, all brightly colored, flashy displays of the best the places had to offer. Peppering the wall between them were darts sticking out at all sorts of wild angles, as if she'd thrown them from various positions in the room.

Smack dab in the middle of the display one of the darts had hit. He stepped closer and tugged the projectile out, eyeing where it had pierced the second *a* in Atlanta. But where the other darts had entered the wall at an angle, this one appeared to have been deliberately put there, the pin deeply embedded.

He turned toward the sink where a box of unopened hair dye waited. Vibrant Auburn, the top read.

"I'm ready," Liz said from behind him.

Out of her line of vision, he tugged the Atlanta brochure from the wall and stuffed it into his jeans pocket. Then he briefly closed his eyes, almost afraid to find out what new way she had discovered to torture him. Clutching the darts in his hands, he slowly turned, letting out an audible breath when he found her dressed in a pair of baggy khaki shorts and a beige tank top, a crisp white blouse worn loosely over it.

Thong. The word popped into his head as he recalled exactly what Liz Braden had on under all those respectable clothes.

She grabbed her purse then faltered, catching sight of the darts he held. "What are you doing with those?"

He frowned. "I think the question here is what are *you* doing with these?"

"I'm not doing anything," she said, taking them away from him. "At least not anymore."

The high color in her cheeks told him all he needed to know: she had used the darts to choose her next point of destination.

He jostled her toward the door, made her lock up, then ushered her into the truck cab.

He tightly gripped the steering wheel to prevent the truck from bouncing out of one of the potholes directly into the thick brush on either side of the narrow drive.

"You know, you really should get somebody other than Old Man Peabody to look after this place for you," he said, trying to find a safe subject. She wasn't gone yet. And he'd be damned if he didn't try every trick in the book to get her to stay. He glanced over to find her tempting Goliath into her lap. The dog only too willingly agreed and blissfully tilted his head back to allow her to scratch his chin.

"Better yet, you should sell it," he said.

Out of the corner of his eye, he watched her cease movement. Goliath whined, upset by the cessation of attention.

Bull's-eye.

"Sell it?" she fairly croaked.

He nodded slowly. He'd long suspected that Liz hung on to the house as a safety net. Hell, even he'd clung to her ownership, hoping she'd someday come back. The mere prospect of her selling her grandmother's old place, cutting off all ties to Manchester, might be just the splash of cold water she needed to help her realize she didn't want to leave at all.

The stunned, hurt expression on her face nearly made him regret the suggestion, despite his intentions. Nearly, but not quite.

"If you're honest about your need to move on, to leave Manchester, then why are you hanging on to this old, decaying piece of the past?" He looked at her meaningfully. "Unless, of course, you do plan to stay."

Absently, she drew her fingers down Goliath's back, her gaze fixed on Mitch's face.

"You want me to sell the house?" she asked again.

He closely guarded his expression to keep his amusement from showing through. Looked like Liz wasn't the only one good at manipulation. "If you're leaving, then yes," he said finally. "Yes, Liz, I think you should sell the house."

He made a conscious effort to ease back his foot from the gas pedal. A dull pang of fear assaulted his stomach as he considered the possibility of her taking him up on his suggestion. The mere thought of the pile of lumber behind them not belonging to Liz anymore... Well, he only hoped he hadn't taken this thing too far.

HE WANTS ME to sell the house.

She really didn't know why his words bothered her so. But they did. Up until that point, she'd never really thought about Gran's place much. It was enough that she always knew it was there. Sell it? She'd never even considered the option. She absently scrubbed under Goliath's ears. She supposed circumstances might be different if she needed the money. But she didn't. Well, at least she wouldn't as soon as she had access to her accounts, which shouldn't be too much longer now.

Before she knew it, the McCoy place came into view. She scanned it, again noting the changes, yet cherishing the things that had stayed the same. She'd never thought of herself as particularly sentimental. Of course, there had been little opportunity for such emotion given her chosen lifestyle. Now? Well, now she found herself sweetly bombarded with all things familiar.

What was it Gran had once said? You always had more fun remembering the events of your life than living them? Was that what was happening now? Was that why she was upset by the prospect of letting her grandmother's house go?

She glanced at Mitch and felt the expected jolt of fiery electricity dance along her nerve endings. Oh, she seemed to be enjoying the present just fine, thank you very much. She could just imagine what she would feel when she looked back on this brief time with Mitch again.

She wasn't sure what made this time different, somehow better, than when they'd been together before. Maybe it was because they'd finally slept together. Or perhaps they'd both grown up during their time apart. Yes, she'd loved Mitch then. But there had been so much uncertainty. So much about herself she didn't know and needed to find out.

Now....

Her throat tightened. Now, she suspected that love had never truly gone away. It had stayed locked up in a secret place in her heart, waiting until this moment to spring out and surprise her with its potency. The only problem was that in order to keep the woman she'd become intact, she had to move on. So much of her depended on her work. And Manchester just wasn't big enough to support her career.

"Your father's done a lot of work on this place, hasn't he?" she said, clearing her throat.

"Pops?" Mitch pulled onto the freshly raked, white-gravel drive that led to the house some hundred yards back from the road. "Pops wouldn't care if the ground opened up and swallowed the place whole. I bought my mother's family's part, the Connor division of the spread, from him a month ago, which includes the house. He still lives here, though. And all my brothers come back a lot. As you've already seen." He smiled wryly. "It was the only way my four brothers would tolerate the house changing hands, even though they had no interest in the money pit, as they call it."

She blinked. "This place is yours?"

"Yep. All one hundred and sixty-four acres of it."

Her hand halted on Goliath's soft fur. "I don't remembering it being that big."

"That's because it wasn't. Connor objected to my purchas-

ing the McCoy part, which granddad used to farm, so I
bought a large annex from the neighbors on the other side."

"Connor didn't want you to buy the old McCoy stretch? Is
that house really still there? It was practically falling down
when we were kids." She vaguely recalled it was miles on
the other side of the property. It had taken her and Mitch
nearly all morning to hike there once. Then neither one of
them had had the guts to go inside. With its sun-bleached exterior and broken windows, she'd been convinced it was
haunted. Needless to say, they'd never gone back.

"Yeah, it's still standing—barely—and, yeah, Connor objected. We're all still trying to figure that one out."

He pulled up to the side door of the impressive, two-story
structure that was part of the old Connor spread and shut off
the engine. Liz stared up at the house. What would Mitch
want with such a huge place? From what she could piece together from memory, there were at least six bedrooms upstairs, a den, a full-sized family room, a sitting room she'd
never entered, along with a formal dining room and an eat-
in kitchen downstairs....

She turned back to find him watching her, the expression
on his face curious.

"What?" she asked.

His grin made her go soft inside. "Nothing. Come on."

Liz followed him from the cab of the truck, holding the
door so Goliath could jump out after her. She reached down
and patted the dog, then he ran off toward the opposite side
of the parking area. She watched him go, spotting a large
fenced-in area where a mismatched menagerie of animals
stood at attention, some wagging tails big and small, others
chomping at the metal links penning them in.

She counted two goats, a mule, a pig, a St. Bernard and a
cow, while just outside the fence lay three overfed cats, sun-
ning themselves.

Mitch stepped over to the fence and fed the mule something from a bucket hanging on a nearby post. She could practically see his broad shoulders relax.

"I'm beginning to think I should start calling this place The Final Pasture," he murmured, drawing his fingers along the sleek nose of the mule. "I don't have any of these animals by choice. One of the goats I took off the neighbor's hands about a month ago when he said he couldn't handle him anymore. The mule came from Old Man Klammer. After that, it seemed everybody in town had an unwanted animal they needed to unload." He gestured toward the cats. "The black one I found in a box near the curb a couple of days ago, along with her six kittens." He scanned the freshly mown grass. "The little devils should be around here someplace. Sheba never leaves them too far behind."

"Sheba?"

"Yeah. You only have to watch her for a while to figure that one out." His grin rivaled the brightness of the sun shining over his shoulder. "If you're good, maybe I'll tell you the rest of their names."

Liz shaded her eyes with her hand, an agreeable tranquillity flowing through her. "So, time's a-tickin'. What did you want to show me?"

His grin widened. "Follow me."

12

HE HAD HIS WORK cut out for him, that was for sure.

Still, everything was going better than he'd planned so far.

Mitch leaned against the side of the new barn, crossing his legs at the ankles. He took a fresh look around him, drinking in his surroundings through another's eyes, namely, Liz's. And he liked what he saw.

What was not to like? In early July, central Virginia was at her most beautiful. Everything was green and lush. The air was full of the pungent smells of wildflowers and all things growing. The sky bluer than any he'd ever seen, with fluffy white clouds skidding across it. The rolling hills heading off to the west and the magical Blue Ridge Mountains.

He glanced back inside the barn where he'd left Liz patting the old pig he'd agreed to take from Old Man Peabody. He'd given her a tour of the house and quietly, careful not to appear too eager, shared all the plans he had to renovate the interior. He'd taken her out back to where he'd planted a half-assed vegetable garden and watched her pull a couple of weeds from between the crooked rows, her fingers looking at home in the rich earth. Then he'd led her through the barn, ready with the answers to her questions.

She hadn't begun asking those questions yet. But she would. He was sure of it.

When he'd sat down at the kitchen table last night to map out his plan, he'd called it the Seduction of Liz. But far from the physical connotations the title suggested, he was out to seduce her heart. He wanted her to remember that she'd once loved Manchester as much as he did. That she'd once loved him. Still did, if he was any judge of character. But he wasn't about to trust his judgment that far. It was enough to see her responding to his tour in the eat-everything-up way that she responded to everything else. In his estimation, it would only be a matter of time before she realized that this was where she belonged. Here. With him.

And that was his major enemy, wasn't it? Time. He restlessly pushed from the barn. With Ruth back at the diner, Bo soon to follow, Myra returned from her vacation and life pretty much back to normal in town, it was only a matter of time before Liz straightened out whatever mess she'd gotten herself into in Boston and moved on.

He couldn't let that happen.

LIZ LANGUIDLY WALKED down the long aisle of the newly constructed barn in the direction Mitch had gone. She peeked at the stall doors she passed, noticing they weren't mere chains blocking entrance or exit, but solid wood with places for brass nameplates. She slowed her stride and looked inside one, finding a fresh bed of hay blanketing the floor, and what looked like a feed bucket hanging just inside the gate.

A feed bucket? She tucked her hair behind her ear and continued toward the door. Probably where the mule slept.

As she neared the pool of sunlight streaming in from the towering, open doors of the barn, she stopped, her breath catching. The sight of dust motes floating in the shaft of warm light caused a surge of memories to burst forth in her heart rather than her mind. Memories of long, lazy summer days when she and Mitch would walk hand-in-hand in the cornfields, loll about in the grass, feed each other a light lunch Ruth would sometimes put together for them. How long ago that time seemed. Before she had earned her degree. Back before Gran had died. Before Mitch had proposed to her on the front steps of the general store because she'd found the ring in his pocket.

Someone sighed wistfully. She realized it was her. How simple life had been then.

She stepped into the light, then beyond, picking Mitch out instantly, crouched down near the bed of his truck. In one of his large hands were two-black-and-white puffs of fur. He was trying to coax a third out from under the truck with a length of rope.

Liz's stomach did an odd sort of somersault.

As she slowly made her way across the gravel toward him, she wondered exactly what Mitch's agenda was. First he'd suggested she sell Gran's house. Then he was showing her around his. Goliath bounded up to her. She petted him, her gaze fastened on the man across the drive.

Mitch pulled the rope out from under the truck, a brown-and-tan kitten clutched onto the thick cord in a mixture of fear and playfulness.

"There you are, Spike." He picked the tiny thing up with his other hand and brought it eye-to-eye. The kitty batted at his nose. "How many times have I told you and your siblings here that the truck is off limits, hmm? The last thing I want is kitty pancakes." The kitten burrowed into the side of Mitch's face, appearing to hug him close, rather than bat at him. It purred so loudly, Liz could hear it from ten feet away.

Oh, how good Mitch was at making her purr.

She cleared her throat.

Mitch looked over his shoulder at her, his grin widening. She noticed the warmth in his green, green eyes. And for the first time she wished she had a camera, to capture this unguarded moment.

He walked over to the fenced-in area and gently dropped

the kittens inside, watching until they scampered toward their mother, who had eyed the entire rescue operation while bathing herself.

Liz tore her gaze away from his all-too-handsome face, feeling suddenly restless. She admitted to herself that one of the reasons she'd come out here today was to prove to herself that she still didn't belong. That the fears that had racked her seven years ago applied even today. She'd needed to prove to herself she'd done the right thing when she walked out on Mitch McCoy.

But she found comparing today's circumstances to yesterday's impossible. Mitch was no longer an FBI agent prone to long absences due to assignments. And she no longer thought herself a woman with no worth—she'd proven herself very capable of forging a good career and a life for herself...outside Manchester.

She briefly closed her eyes, then opened them again, focusing on the lush grass that seemed to stretch to forever behind the house. She tried to superimpose the image of her office in Boston. An office she would reconstruct in Atlanta. But her mind and heart weren't having any of it.

"Looks like a summer storm is brewing," Mitch said next to her.

Liz checked the southwestern horizon to find dark gray clouds resting on top of a sloping hill. She leaned next to him against the truck. Out of the corner of her eye, she caught him crossing his arms over his green-cotton-covered chest.

There were a few things that didn't completely jibe. Why would Mitch want to put fences up along his property line? Certainly he wasn't afraid of his crops running off. She absently rubbed her arms. Then again, she hadn't noticed any crops. When he'd said he'd bought his father's property, she had assumed he would take up farming. But she'd spotted no neat rows of corn dotting the horizon, or small, leafy bean plants covering the brown earth like nature's blanket. In fact, if she wasn't mistaken, the only thing planted was grass. Grass that appeared to have been mowed. She could imagine the size of *that* lawn mower.

"You're up to something, McCoy. I haven't figured out what yet. But I will."

"I don't know what you mean."

She smiled. "Sure you don't." She crossed her arms loosely under her breasts. He watched the movement a little too closely. "Tell me this, Mitch. You're a P.I. now, right? What, are you on vacation? Between jobs or something?"

He chuckled. "I'm more than between jobs, Liz. I'm retired. I still hold interest in a partnership in D.C. and I held on to a couple clients, but otherwise I'm...free."

She eyed him standing in the direct sunlight. Damn the man, but he looked better than any man had a right to. The breeze brought his soapy scent to her nose, his skin smelling as good as it had when he'd picked her up that morning.

It was then she put her finger directly on what was bothering her: her lack of knowledge of him. Not knowing what made him tick now. She'd been so wrapped up in stringing him along, struggling with her physical needs for him, she hadn't taken a closer look at him and what he'd become, beyond the obvious. But this uninterrupted time was giving her plenty of room to get to know this new Mitch. And she found herself more drawn to him than ever.

He gestured toward the truck. "Ready?"

She glanced at the red vehicle. "What? Day over already?"

"Oh, no. It's just getting started, angel."

She felt a peculiar little flutter in her belly as he put Goliath in the pen with the rest of the animals, then helped her into the cab. She flipped the sun-visor down and clicked open the vanity mirror. She noticed a smudge across the bridge of her nose. Now how had that gotten there?

Mitch climbed in next to her. The engine hummed to life.

He sat for a long moment, staring at her, then reached out a hand and thumbed her nose. She automatically tried to tug her head away from him, but he caught her chin.

"Would you hold on a minute?" he said, his voice rough and low. "I'm trying to get something off."

Liz held her head still, watching him dampen his thumb with his tongue, then rub at the spot on her nose. She fastened her gaze on his inviting mouth and wondered at the heavy staccato beat of her heart.

"Are you done yet? For God's sake, it can't be that big," she croaked. Another moment of him touching her, no matter how innocent the purpose, and she was afraid she'd straddle him right where he sat.

He drew his hand away and chuckled. "Guess I'm as done as I'm going to get, huh?"

Mitch backed out of the spot near the house. But instead of heading for the driveway and the road beyond, he pointed the nose of the truck in the direction of the fields behind the house. Liz gasped and grabbed the dash as the wheels left the gravel and bounced along the uneven grassland.

Surprised laughter burst from her throat. "Mitch! What are you doing?"

"You'll see soon enough. Why don't you just sit back and enjoy the ride?"

She flattened one of her hands on the ceiling of the cab to prevent her head from hitting the roof. How many acres had he said he had? One hundred and sixty or thereabouts? Why did she have the feeling he was going to ride over every single foot of that acreage?

And why in the hell was she liking it so much?

MITCH PATTED a spot next to him on the red-and-white checked blanket he'd spread beneath the overhang of trees.

Liz caught her lip between her teeth, looking at him as if torn between wanting to make a sassy remark and needing to run.

"Don't tell me, McCoy. You have this picnic fantasy you want to play out."

He breathed a sigh of relief when the sassy remark won out. "Yep. And I've cast you in the starring role."

Her laugh was low and raspy as she sat down next to him. "I haven't been on a picnic since..."

Mitch opened the wicker basket Ruth had helped him put together that morning. He'd been banking on her not having been on a picnic for as long as he had—which would make it the week before their wedding seven years ago. He remembered that afternoon all too clearly. Not because of what was to come, but because they'd come very close to breaking their vow to wait until their wedding night.

He willed his growing erection away and reached into the basket.

"It's been a while for me, too," he said.

All her favorites. He'd gone all out to make sure he had every last one of them. Lasagna in a warmer. Greens with olive oil and lemon. Fruity red wine. Crusty baguettes and soft white cheese. Tapioca. Everything a growing girl needed. He swept his gaze over her body where she rested back on her elbows, her ankles crossed over the edge of the blanket.

For long minutes neither of them said anything. Merely passed the dishes to each other and slowly devoured the food he'd brought along. Afterward, Liz helped him clean up, then lay against the blanket, staring up through the swaying tree branches.

He lay back with her.

"Now I'm really suspicious," she said quietly.

Mitch drank in her profile, wondering at the serious shadow in her hazel eyes. "Oh?"

She turned her head toward him. "One of the first pieces of advice I give to my clients is know your market. Be sure you know what you're selling, then package your product accordingly. Then target that market head-on."

He grinned. "I'm not selling anything, Liz."

She was silent as her gaze slowly scanned his features. "Oh, but you are, Mitch."

He folded his hands behind his head. "Maybe it's the wine, but I don't think I'm following you. What product? And what market am I targeting?"

In direct contrast to her serious tone, she got up on all fours, then straddled him. The feel of her soft feminine parts pressing against his hard—and growing harder all the time—male parts made him groan. She smiled and squeezed her thighs together.

"I find I can explain myself better if I have the audience's undivided attention."

Oh, she had his attention all right. But he didn't think it was where she wanted it. He fought to keep his hands behind his head. Then again, maybe this tactic was purely diversionary in nature. If so, he was in deep trouble. Because with her moving her hips in that rhythmic way, he wasn't sure how long he'd be able to decipher her words.

A crack of thunder sounded off in the distance.

"Go on," he croaked rather than said.

"You see, I knew you were up to something, but I wasn't exactly sure what. At least not until you brought me here and opened that damn picnic basket."

She ran her hand down his T-shirt-covered abdomen, then slid it between them. Through the thick denim of his jeans, she found his erection, then positioned it so it ran the length of his zipper. She resettled herself, his hard shaft lining up neatly with the juncture between her legs. He watched her moisten her lips with the tip of her tongue and groaned.

"You've lost me again," he said, commanding himself to concentrate on what she was saying rather than what she was doing.

"All my favorites were in that basket, McCoy." She ground against him. Her shudder nearly shattered his best intentions.

"Your favorites...."

"Uh-huh." She braced her hands against his shoulders, her hair tumbling around her face. "You see, in that one moment, everything came together." His gaze flicked to where her breasts pressed against the thin cotton of her tank top. "I figured out that I'm the target audience." His control was dwindling fast. "And you're the product."

Liz's head felt light from the wine, her body on fire from being provocatively pressed against Mitch, but neither state completely stopped her thought processes. And she'd concluded that Mitch was playing her as adeptly as she'd been playing him this past week.

Thing about it was, his actions excited her all the more.

She leaned down and ran the tip of her tongue along his lower lip. When he tried to kiss her, she pulled away.

"Product?" he repeated.

"Uh-huh." She leaned down again, pressing her lips against first one temple, then the other. Mercy, he tasted good. "Only thing is—" she pulled back, directly meeting his gaze "—you don't have to sell yourself to me, McCoy. I already have my money out and ready."

Before she could blink, he had rolled her over onto her back. If there was such a thing as two people fitting perfectly together, then they were it. His hips fit just so between her thighs. His height was just right to allow him to kiss her while he also saw to other things.

He hungrily claimed her mouth, then pulled back. "Problem is, Liz, I'm not exactly sure what you're buying."

She tightened her legs around his waist. "This." She reveled in the sound of his deep groan.

He cupped her breast through her tank top. She caught her breath as she stared into the intoxicating depths of his eyes and heard him whisper, "That's not all I'm selling."

She kept her eyes open and watchful as he again dipped his head toward hers. She was still as he licked one side of her mouth, then the other. But when he fastened his lips over hers, she completely lost herself in his kiss, instantly forgetting why she had felt that momentary pang of panic.

Moments later, rain channeled through the sieve of the tree branches above them. For long moments, neither of them noticed—until a deafening crack of thunder sounded directly overhead. Reluctantly pulling apart, they gathered everything together and dashed for the truck.

13

MITCH GROUND the truck to a halt near the side door, shut it off and together they made a run for the small overhang protecting the steps from the elements. Liz felt the drop in temperature as she followed him through the mudroom into the kitchen of the large old house. Central air. She trembled. Not because it was too cold, but because her skin was damp. On the wall, she barely registered an old aerial picture of the house, likely shot from a crop duster.

"I plan to get an after shot taken once I get everything in order," Mitch murmured.

Liz shivered, finding his words didn't have to go too far to drift into her ear. He stood mere inches, if that, away from her backside, his breath teasing her neck.

"Order?"

"Uh-huh."

His nearness blocked out everything but the sensual heat that radiated from his tall, rock-solid frame behind her. He reached around her to open a drawer. The movement brought him flush against her, his erection pressing insistently against her bottom. Liz caught her breath, nearly groaning when he took two tea towels from the drawer then turned her around. Her gaze was riveted to the droplets of water clinging to his lashes while he languidly drew the soft terry along the side of her neck. The searing hunger in his eyes multiplied her state of arousal tenfold. Her knees weakened and she leaned back against the counter for support.

"Mitch?" she whispered, staring at his tempting mouth, longing clenching her stomach.

"What?"

He drew nearer and she swallowed hard, her heart pounding an uneven rhythm in her chest. "Do you have a thing for counters?"

His advance halted and his gaze flicked up to her eyes. "I'm thinking I must."

She parted her lips in anticipation of his kiss, a shudder running through her as a loud roar of thunder shook the floor beneath her feet.

"Me, too—"

His mouth descended on hers, trapping whatever other words she might have uttered under the welcome weight of his kiss.

A moan surged up Liz's raw throat. He tasted of red wine and smelled of soap, but the feel of his powerful body crowded against hers was one hundred percent pure Mitch McCoy.

A welcome shiver skittered across her skin as she wound her arms around his waist and dug her fingers into the flesh of his back through his T-shirt. Swiftly, his kiss grew more exacting, more dominating, seeking a response she was only too willing to give. Arching into him, she wanted more than the limited embrace allowed. Dragging her fingers down the length of his back to his sculpted rear, she pulled briefly away from the kiss, drawing a ragged breath.

Holding her gaze, Mitch nudged her knees apart with one of his, sliding his leg between hers. She whimpered deep in her throat, a slow burn starting at the contact of his leg against her pelvis. He tangled his hands in her hair, hauling her mouth back to his, his tongue delving deeper, challenging hers to a duel of passions.

She jerked her hands to his abdomen and restlessly tugged

his wet shirt from the waist of his jeans, stopping only when her fingers rested against the hard, hot surface of his chest. The coarse hair felt marvelously tantalizing as she inched her fingertips toward his nipples, feeling them harden beneath her attention. Pulling her mouth from his, she fastened her lips around a tiny nub, generously laving one, then the other, reveling in the soft groan of pleasure she coaxed from him.

"Get up here," he demanded, grasping her shoulders and forcing her to eye level.

Her chest rapidly rose and fell as she drank in the devilish gleam in his intoxicating green eyes. She curved her fingers halfway around his thick, pulsing erection, frustrated by the heavy denim preventing her from making closer contact.

She heard the tearing of fabric, and jerked to find Mitch drawing the sleeve of her shirt down her arms, and ripping her tank top loose, gazing hungrily at the flesh he revealed inch by inch. He halted when the material skimmed over and past her right breast, exposing her frilly white bra, her pale pink aureole clearly visible through the lacy fabric. She pulled in a ragged breath, watching as he hesitantly brought his hand within millimeters of cupping her, then drew away.

When he fastened his mouth over her breast through the fabric, she gasped.

Unbearable heat gushed through her limbs, coalescing in a monstrous pool in her lower abdomen. She moaned and pressed herself more powerfully against his leg, relishing the delicious emotion taking possession of her.

Another tear and her back-fastening bra popped open in the front. Through lowered lids, she watched him stare at her, grinning mischievously. "I always end up ruining your clothes, don't I, angel?" he murmured, running his hot tongue from one of her hardened nipples to the other, devouring both in one ravenous sweep.

An answering reply was on the tip of her tongue, but

never made it past her lips as he thrust his leg more fully against her. She nearly shattered, gripping his shoulders to steady herself as he boldly plucked at her aching nipples.

The raw yearning that transformed his face as he gazed at her sent a new sensation skating down her spine—the powerful sensation of knowing she could imbue so much longing in him with merely a look. He slid his hands up from her waist, probing her rib cage, curving his fingers under each of her breasts and lifting them, marveling at the gentle slope of her tender flesh. Bringing his lips down, he covered her right nipple, tugging it into the depths of his mouth where his tongue stroked it.

The heat puddled in Liz's stomach changed into a terrible ache as the fingers of his free hand trailed a path down to her shorts. He lessened the pressure of his leg so he could outline the triangle of her engorged womanhood with his fingers. Liz bit down on her bottom lip, trying to slow down her climax, needing to wait until he could join her to give herself over to the delicious paroxysm.

When he cupped her in his palm and squeezed, her restraint vanished.

Liz exploded, liquid heat flooding her body. She gasped in shock, writhing restlessly against him, thrusting her hands into his hair, pulling him closer, needing him closer still.

Her quivers subsided and she lessened the grip on his hair. He lifted to gaze at her, his eyes full of devilment.

"Nice to know some things never change," he murmured, flicking his tongue out and across her upper lip. "I could always make you come apart with one touch."

She nipped at him but he drew his tongue back into his mouth and grinned.

"Oh, but Mitch," she murmured, "I'm hoping you're going to do a whole lot more than touch me now."

His grin expanded and he hastily kissed her, then kissed her again.

"You have no idea," he whispered, wrapping his arms around her and thrusting the ridge of his arousal fully against her.

She shuddered and ripped at his shirt, yanking it halfway up only to restlessly abandon it to grope for the metal button of his jeans. Within moments, she had it undone.

His deep chuckle tickled her ear and he caught her hands. She stared at him, puzzled, until he broke away and started to lead her from the room.

Liz saw little on their rushed trip up the stairs to his old bedroom. She had a quick glimpse of an iron bedstead covered in a stitched, white coverlet, and four large windows that overlooked the front of the property, before he virtually flung her to the bed, then lunged on top of her.

The old bedsprings groaned beneath their combined weight, and Mitch grinned.

"You don't know how long I've fantasized about this," he murmured, catching her right earlobe between his teeth. "About having you stretched beneath me, just like this, on this bed." He slid the tip of his tongue inside her ear, causing her to wriggle fitfully against him. "Wondering what the springs would sound like when we made love."

Made love....

The words warmly invaded Liz's clouded mind. She savored the feel of him on top of her, forcing the air from her lungs, bracketing her body with his arms.

"Of course," he began, drawing back from her, "in my fantasies you're naked."

A low laugh vibrated her stomach. "That's easily fixed, you know."

He grinned.

She's incredible, Mitch thought, reluctantly rolling off her to lie on his side. He propped his head on his hand. Everything about Liz was incredible. From her magnificent blond hair, down to her purple toenails, she was one remarkable piece of work.

Teasingly reaching out, he peeled away what little remained of her top and her bra, then undid her belt. Flicking a gaze up to where she watched him with a sort of detached wonder, he slowly, with some help from her, dragged her shorts down past her slender hips, and over her legs, his gaze following his movements. He tossed the khaki material to the floor, then trailed his gaze back up to the naughty underwear she'd given him a flash of that morning. A streak of lightning brightened the dim bedroom, illuminating every precious millimeter of her. The resulting rumble of thunder mirrored the need coiling within him.

She squeezed her thighs together and shuddered, but he refused to let her stay that way for long, no matter how much he liked watching her. He spanned his fingers over her right knee, then slid them inward and upward, over the velvet of her inner thigh, and gently forced her legs apart. She hesitated, and he feared she might close them again, but then she relaxed, opening more than her body to him.

His hardened shaft twitched against his stomach as he stared at the scrap of lace and satin barely covering the dusky wedge of her womanhood before disappearing into the enticing crevice between her cheeks. *Oh, my, these things should be illegal.* Restraining himself, he hooked his index finger under the flimsy side string and tugged, fascinated, as she arched her back to make his task easier.

The moment the thong bikini hung from his finger well away from her lush, slick body, she curled against him, forcing him onto his back where she straddled him.

"I think you've stolen my reputation as a tease," she

rasped, her hazel eyes wide and enchanting as she fumbled for his zipper.

She recklessly jerked his T-shirt, jeans and briefs off, her hot gaze taking in every inch of his exposed body from where she still hovered above him.

She began to straddle him again and he quickly grasped her wrists.

"Uh-uh, angel. This time I want to start things the old-fashioned way."

The fierce expression on her bewitching face told him he was in for an argument. He quickly flipped her over and covered the length of her. To circumvent the debate, he slid his fingers down the satiny skin of her belly, simultaneously claiming her mouth with his, swallowing her gasp as he probed her soft curls. Catching the velvety bud between his thumb and forefinger, he gently squeezed. She bucked from the mattress so wildly, he thought he'd caused her to climax again. But she was reaching for him, thrashing against him, drawing him nearer.

"Please...no more teasing," she whispered urgently. "I...can't take any more."

Slipping his fingers into her sleek aperture, his own body shuddered as he found her more than ready for him.

The shudder melted into a quake as she wrapped her fingers around his erection, grazing her thumb against the length before guiding him to press against her.

Reaching for and finding the box Jake had left for him, he quickly sheathed himself with a purple condom. Then he coaxed her open, clenching his teeth as her moist satin heat closed around the tip of his shaft. Exquisite sensation swelled through his body, and he grasped her hips, holding her still even as she strained upward against him. She was so exceptionally tight, so remarkably sleek.

He increased his grip on her hips and she whimpered,

begging him to enter her more deeply, to satisfy the hunger raging through them both. In one smooth move, he granted her wish and plunged nearly all the way in, until he reminded himself that she needed time to grow accustomed to him.

She grasped his buttocks, pressing him down, her legs tangling with his, trying to force a deeper union. He gazed into her passion-glazed eyes and the jumble of hair around her face, thinking she truly was an angel. Shaping her wet mouth with his, he slid even deeper into her velvety depths, trapping her moans with his mouth, basking in the overpowering feeling of her surrounding him. Her sweet smell, her roving hands, her inviting body....

He released her hips and groaned when she thrust up against him with such urgency he almost lost it. It took every bit of his self-control not to give in to the glorious emotions roaring inside him as powerfully as the thunderstorm raged outside. But this slow stuff was not getting them anywhere. He withdrew halfway, then thrust into her with such abandon a sob ripped from her throat. Instantly, he feared he had hurt her. Then she gazed up at him and smiled, straining to meet him halfway when he withdrew again.

Together, they set a wild pace to their lovemaking, his ears filled with her passionate cries, his fingers stroking the soft flesh of her breasts, his mouth hungrily pulling at hers, his back enduring the sometimes violent grate of her nails. As the storm outside grew in intensity, so did his thrusts, a ball of fire amassing, burning a savage hole in his stomach, the pressure in his groin building to aching potency. No longer able to restrain the rush of climax, he grasped her hips and tilted them upward, allowing him to plunge deeper, farther. Her answering cry crowded all coherent thought from his mind and his muscles went rigid, held in awe of the feel of her convulsing profoundly around him, compelling him to

fill her, demanding he follow her into the incandescent light
that eclipsed all semblance of sanity.

As the shuddering of their bodies slowly subsided, and
their gasps for air became manageable, Mitch lifted to stare
into her face, smoothing her golden hair back. Her red lips
looked well-kissed, her hazel eyes glowed in the aftermath of
their lovemaking. She smiled, running her fingers over his
sweat-dampened chest, down to where they were still
joined.

"You know, sex like that is almost enough to keep me
here," she whispered, lifting to press her lips gently against
his.

He earnestly studied her in the dim light. "And if I told
you I loved you?"

Outside the thunderstorm had passed, and the only
sounds in the room were the lazy rubbing of her leg against
his, and the ticking of his wind-up alarm clock.

He held his breath. Waited for her answer. This was it.
This was the moment when he'd learn if she was his completely.

"Well," she said slowly, "I don't know, Mitch. Why don't
you tell me and find out?"

She flexed her inner muscles around him and he groaned,
feeling his erection grow within her.

She smiled wickedly, curving her fingers over his buttocks.

I just did tell you, his mind said even as his body took over.
But he couldn't be sure if he'd said the words or not.

She pushed a fresh condom into his hands, then rolled
over and got up onto all fours, straining her lush bottom
against him. It was all he could do to shakily change the condom before thrusting into her with wild abandon.

This time there was no waiting, no hesitant attempt to take
it slowly. He plunged deeply, reveling in the feel of her

straining against him, taking every bit of him into her. He slid his hands to her shoulders, guiding her in a provocative rhythm. Through half-closed lids, he observed himself delving into her velvety heat, then retreating. He dragged his fingers down the column of her spine, watching as she automatically arched her back, her silken hair creating a fringed, golden curtain over her flawless skin. Clutching her hips fiercely, he gave himself over to the sensations pulsing through him, thrusting into her again and again until the world exploded in a bolt of wondrous, white light.

LIZ SLUGGISHLY DRAGGED herself out of the haze of slumber, the mattress beneath her unfamiliarly soft, the play of light on the opposite wall foreign. Next to her lay something warm and furry. At her start, Goliath whimpered, then licked her face. She sat up and the crisp sheet fell to her waist. A waist free of clothes, her bare breasts shimmering in the dim light wafting in through the windows.

"Mitch?" she whispered, finding the other side of the bed empty.

She hesitantly lay back down, not wanting to disturb the languid tranquillity saturating her tired muscles. Draping an arm across Goliath's back, she smiled, luxuriously reviewing the past few hours she and Mitch had shared...and back farther, to when she first returned to Manchester.

When she'd arrived, she remembered wondering if fate had somehow intervened in her life by tugging Mitch back into it.

She laughed quietly and closed her eyes, recalling the array of animals that called the new barn their home, the fence he was erecting around his property, the horse-breeding operation she suspected he planned to start. So different from the cold one she had forged for herself, his was a wonderful, seductive life full of peace and peppered with the excitement provided by the town's distinctive population.

It was a life she was growing to love more than she ever had before.

She went still, expecting the anxiety that had plagued her her entire life to claim her, the dubious voice in her head to tell her she didn't fit in, didn't belong here. Didn't belong anywhere.

The apprehension never came as she stared at the ceiling, transfixed. Is this where she belonged? Could this be the place she had always been destined to settle? The same place she had run away from so many years before?

After fighting the idea for so long, she found the concept incredible, astonishing.

Suddenly restless, she swung her feet to the floor and rummaged around for her panties. She came across Mitch's T-shirt and tugged that on as well, then padded toward one of the windows, open, letting in a muggy, after-storm breeze.

Shivering, she pushed aside the sheer, jumping when she spotted Mitch sitting on a stretch of tin roofing on top of the front porch overhang.

"Mitch?" she whispered. "What are you doing out here?"

He didn't answer. Instead, he scooted to the side, indicating she was welcome to join him.

Glancing down at his T-shirt skimming her thighs, then out to him wearing only his jeans, she carefully climbed through the window. The roof didn't slope much, just enough to let the rain run off, and the tin sheeting was cool and dry under her bare feet. She crouched down, tugging the cotton shirt to protect her bottom before sitting.

Resting her back against the house, she felt a rush of recklessness, of doing something outside the norm and having it appeal to her. Nearby, male crickets chirped, and the sweet, heavy scent of honeysuckle filled her senses. She smiled and shifted her head to stare at him.

She wanted to reach for his hand, but saw that he had both of them locked between his bent knees.

The crescent of moon winked out from behind a wisp of cloud, bathing the horizon in its silvery glow. Liz wondered at the furtive quality of the light, the way it outlined the trees and kissed the rolling hills like a fleeting lover. She sighed.

"This is nice." A sated yawn seized her and she quietly laughed. "How long was I asleep?"

He shrugged. "An hour or two."

She stared at him. "Have you been out here that long?"

"Nearly." He dragged in a breath and released it.

She looked back at the horizon, for the first time truly opening her heart to the stretch of land, much as she had opened herself to the man next to her. The sensation proved remarkably liberating, imbuing her with the strength of belonging.

She sensed his gaze on her and she turned to look at him. "What?" she asked, her cheeks heating as she fluffed her sleep-rumpled hair. "I look awful, don't I?"

He said nothing for a long moment, his eyes black in the silvery light. Finally, he shook his head. "No, Liz, you don't look awful. You look beautiful."

Which was part of the problem, wasn't it? Mitch thought. Liz had always been, and always would be, beautiful to him.

"What, exactly, do you have planned for the land?" She rubbed her palm against the edge of his T-shirt. "I mean, I didn't see any farm equipment in the new barn, and it's obvious you didn't plant this year." She looked at him. "Then there's the fence...."

He raked his gaze over her flushed face, but said nothing.

He'd thought she'd remember, if given the chance. Maybe he'd been wrong. They'd only talked once about his dreams while meandering through the neighbor's cornfields at harvest time. He might recall the conversation word for word, but there was no reason for her to remember it at all. After all this time and everything that had happened, perhaps it had been unreasonable to expect her to know what he had in mind.

"You're going to breed horses, aren't you?" she said, breaking the silence.

He relaxed against the house and grinned. "Yes."

She smiled back at him.

His grin slowly ebbed. Over the past eight months, all he'd planned, he'd planned to do alone. He hadn't counted on Liz rolling back into town. And he hadn't planned on loving her again. And with that love came the instant insertion of her into every aspect of his life. While touring the house, he'd readily discarded his ideas for decorating and instead wondered which color scheme and designs she would choose. He'd found himself thinking how his mother's old sewing room with the window facing the east would make a great nursery. When they'd toured the barn, he noticed how the back room would make a wonderful office for her to run the business end of things.

He tunneled his fingers through his hair restlessly. When he'd told her he loved her, she hadn't directly responded. Rather, she'd turned the tables back on him, then made sure he couldn't pursue the matter by distracting him with sex.

What she *had* said continued to demand examination: "Sex like that is almost enough to make me stay."

Almost.

Maybe it was long past time to admit that nothing could keep her here. That the ace he thought he'd held by opening up his life and dreams to her had turned out to be a powerless joker. And as soon as he figured out how to clear up the trouble she was in, she would drive out of town as easily as she had driven back in.

He couldn't believe he'd been so stupid. Again.

"Mitch? Is something wrong?"

"Wrong?" he repeated. "Yes. I suppose you could say that." *Talk about understatements.* He looked her full in the face. "Don't you think it's time you stopped stringing me along? Tell me, Liz, what in the hell are you running from in Boston?"

Her sexy smile threatened to chase all thought from his head. He battled the urge to haul her back inside and forget about why she was here. Forget about Boston and when she was going to leave. But he couldn't. Not anymore.

"I can't believe you're still worrying about that."

"Yes, well, I am. And I think it's time for you to give me reason to stop."

Twin beams of light cut through the darkness. He looked toward the road to find a car pulling up into the driveway, illuminating them where they sat on the roof. Liz tugged at the hem of her T-shirt and he cursed. Hell of a time for Pops to decide to come home.

The car stopped.

"That you, Liz?" his father called as if he'd just run into her on the street. "I'd heard you were in Manchester. Welcome home."

"Thanks, Mr. McCoy," she said.

The old man put his sedan into gear, continued up the drive and parked.

"I think we've just been busted," Liz whispered, leaning into him.

Mitch didn't respond. Couldn't respond.

"Is something wrong?" she asked quietly.

Everything's wrong, Mitch wanted to say. Instead, he

stood up and offered her his hand. "Come on. Let's get you home."

MITCH WASN'T SURPRISED to find Pops waiting up for him when he returned from dropping Liz off. He stepped into the kitchen, acknowledged him with a nod, then poured himself a cup of the coffee that was always on the warmer when his father was home.

"Seems like old times, eh?" Sean McCoy said, taking a long sip from his own cup.

"Excuse me if I don't feel like talking right now, Pops. All I want to do is go to sleep."

With a move of his foot under the table, Sean pushed a chair toward him. "From what I can gather, you've been getting as much sleep as I have lately—which ain't much. Sit down."

Mitch looked at him over the rim of his cup, then sighed and took the chair. Saying goodnight to Liz without revealing what was going through his mind had to be one of the hardest things he'd ever done, especially since she was an expert at noticing change in demeanor. And, boy, had his demeanor taken a notable nosedive.

"So what's up?" Pops asked.

Mitch scrubbed his face with his hand. "Let's just say things are resembling old times a little too much."

"Ah." Sean sat back, looking at nothing in particular.

Mitch sat back as well, quietly examining his father. He'd been wanting to turn to him for counsel ever since Liz's return. This wasn't exactly what he'd had in mind. "Ah? Is that all you have to say?"

Sean shrugged. "Don't know that there's much more to say."

The house was quiet, nothing but the sound of the light summer breeze occasionally billowing the kitchen curtains, now that he'd turned off the air-conditioning and opened all the windows.

Maybe Pops was right. Maybe there wasn't much more to say. He'd known going into this that Liz's leaving was a probability more than a possibility. And when he'd made the decision to convince her to stay, he'd done so knowing his chances of success were marginal.

Still, it had been so easy for him to dupe himself into believing he'd made a difference. That her passionate responses to him were a sign that she was coming around. That this time they could make it work.

His chair legs screeched against the tile as he shifted uneasily.

He looked at his father. He needed something, anything, to get his mind off his own problems. "So what's been up with you?" he asked, figuring turnabout was fair play. Besides, Pops looked about as good as he felt.

Sean shrugged. "Not much."

Mitch grasped his coffee cup. "Could have fooled me. As much as you've been around here lately, I'd say a lot was up."

"*Was* being the key word."

He hiked a brow. It was then he realized Pops had made it home the past few nights. A little late, and he'd been gone even before Mitch got up in the morning. But he'd been home.

He took a long sip of coffee. Was it him, or was this conversation strange? Him and his father both down in the dumps because of women?

Mitch cleared his throat. No matter how uncomfortable it made him, he at least owed Pops a show of sympathy. "I'm sorry things didn't work out. You know. Between you and your...um, lady friend."

The sparkle of amusement returned to Sean's blue eyes.

"Who said they didn't work out?" He ran a callused thumb over the rim of his cup. "Sorry to disappoint you, boy, but things with me and my 'um, lady friend,' are working out just fine, thanks for asking." His voice lowered. "Too fine, if you ask me."

Mitch grimaced. It was bad enough his father *had* a love life to talk about. That his should be succeeding where his own was not...

He silently cursed. Now what had caused that stupid thought to skid through his mind? "Ah," he said in much the same manner as Sean had.

Pops squinted at him, emphasizing the lines that fanned out from the corners of his eyes. "Now what's that supposed to mean?"

Mitch shrugged. "Oh, nothing. I'm just guessing that your lady friend must be pushing the commitment issue."

"Actually she's not. It's just gotten to that stage, you know, where you either decide to take things further, or you just drop everything altogether. You know?"

Yes, Mitch did know. All too well. "You mean, like letting your families meet each other. Little details like that."

Sean sat back and sighed. "Yeah. Something like that."

Mitch wondered if his father had been taking lessons from Liz on the art of ambiguity. "I don't know what the big deal is. I mean, sure, your seeing someone on the sly was a little surprising to all of us." He cleared his throat. "But if you're serious about this woman, then why don't you just bring her around for dinner one night?"

"It should be so simple." Sean got up and topped off his cup. Mitch waved him away when he moved to do the same to his. He had enough trouble sleeping. "I am assuming that either you or Liz must be pushing the commitment issue at this point." He retook his chair, the squeak of the old wood punctuating his sentence. "My guess is it's you."

"Kind of."

Sean frowned. "Well, either you are or you aren't. Which is it?"

Mitch's fingers tightened around his cup. Distantly he wondered if he could shatter the thick porcelain if he tried hard enough. And whether or not it would make him feel any better. "I've been thinking about, you know, the issue. But I haven't exactly said anything to the other party. At least not in so many words."

Sean merely stared at him. "I won't pretend to know everything that's going on here, Mitch. Because I don't. None of us knows what really happened between you two seven years ago. All I've got to say is that you should stop putt-putting around and use the good sense God gave you."

"Gee, thanks, Pops."

He waved off his remark. "What I mean is, you've got to decide whether or not to tell the woman how you really feel. Or..."

"Or?" Mitch prompted.

"Or live with the consequences."

If only he didn't believe the outcome would be the same either way.

The way he saw it, Liz had already made it plain as day that she was leaving again. He wasn't about to make an even bigger fool out of himself than he had before. Better he should let her think he didn't care one way or another about her leaving. Adios. See ya. It's been nice knowing you again. That kind of thing.

The funny thing was, coming to the decision didn't make him feel any better. But at least he now knew what the future held. And for better or worse, it didn't include Liz.

He got up from the chair. "Thanks, Pops."

Sean blinked at him, clearly confused. "Sure."

14

THE FOLLOWING EVENING, Mitch sat at the counter at Bo and Ruth's Paradise Diner, his jaw clenched so tightly he thought he might grind his teeth to dust. The coffee before him was cold and bitter. And not even Ezra's jubilant disposition as he entertained the people crowding the eatery could lighten the leaden weight crushing his shoulders.

Ruth's dark head appeared in the kitchen window.

"Liz has got to come," she said as Bo stepped up beside her. "She has to or all my planning will be for naught."

"Wouldn't be the first time." Bo grimaced and scratched at a spot near his chest. Ruth swatted him, likely for the comment and for scratching the area that received the majority of the attention following his minor heart attack.

Mitch automatically lifted his coffee cup to his lips, ignoring Ruth's frown as she looked at him. For the past hour, the diner owner had been driving herself crazy with worry over whether or not Liz would swing by as she'd promised. It was all he could do not to remind her that Liz was infamous for not keeping her word.

According to Pops, she had called the house for him twice that day. And had swung by once. He'd been away at the vet's at the time, having taken the six kittens in for their first shots and their mother in to be spayed. Pops had just stared at him expectantly when he'd passed on the news. Mitch hadn't responded, though a part of him had wanted to ask for the details. How had she sounded? Did she leave a specific message?

He grimaced. What was it with him? Psychology had been part of his training at Quantico. He judged himself a hairbreadth away from being classified as some sort of masochist who was co-dependent on Liz's heartbreaking ways. An enabler who allowed Liz back in even knowing she was going to rip out his heart again.

The bell above the door clanged. He turned, half expecting to see Liz breezing in. Instead, he narrowed his gaze on a tall, blond guy who stood just inside the door, looking around the diner. Mitch judged him to be about his own age and height, but that's where the similarities ended. Where he was more comfortable in jeans and T-shirts, this one looked right at home in his dark Brooks Brothers tailored suit. He stiffened, then glanced through the window and caught a glimpse of someone familiar.

Outside stood that damn private investigator from Boston.

The P.I. met his gaze, then ducked off out of the line of vision. A moment later, Liz's old Pacer sputtered and coughed up to the curb.

Mitch absently scratched his head, wondering what the hell was going on. And whether or not he should do anything to stop it.

"Here she comes," Ezra called out.

The instant she entered, the packed diner erupted in a lusty, out-of-tune rendition of "Happy Birthday."

Everyone sang, Mitch noticed, except himself and the newcomer, who stood off to the side, a grin on his face, his arms crossed neatly over his chest.

Who was this guy? And why did he have the feeling he wasn't going to like him?

Liz appeared surprised and touched as Ruth and Bo carried out a gigantic cake in the shape of an angel, halo and all, from the kitchen. Mitch eyed the way the hand she lifted to her mouth trembled as the cake was held out in front of her, and he tensed against the sound of her sexy, throaty laugh.

The singing ended, and after a few robust shouts that she make a wish, silence took over.

And Liz stood completely still. Mitch realized it wasn't because she didn't know what to say, but because she'd noticed the guy standing off to the side.

Mitch shifted on his stool as her gaze sought and then found his. He told himself to turn away. Told himself to keep it light, keep his feelings to himself until after the celebration. But he couldn't. He met her questioning gaze with his stony one. Then he watched her pale.

"Blow out the candles, Liz," Ruth urged.

"Yeah, all thirty of them!" Moses Darton called out.

"You would have to remind me of the number, wouldn't you, Ez?" Liz's gaze flicked around the room, gratitude mingling with confusion in the hazel depths of her eyes. Mitch cleared his throat and stared at his boots, not looking up again until he heard the sound of her blowing out the candles moments later.

Clapping and roars of approval filled the diner and Bo and Ruth shifted to put the cake on a table. Ezra stepped up to Liz, draping an arm over her shoulders.

"I'd like to say one of your birthday gifts is the return on your wager," he said. "But truth is, you lost this time around."

Her gaze snapped to his so quickly, Mitch didn't have time to avoid it. He grimaced and shook his head, trying to dispel the challenge in her eyes by indicating he hadn't said anything. He hadn't had to. Pops hadn't been the only one on the road last night. From what he could gather, the Darton brothers had gotten an eyeful of him kissing Liz goodnight when he'd dropped her off. And they'd told everyone who'd listen.

"Gifts! Gifts!" Myra shouted, giving her friend a bear hug, then thrusting a small package into Liz's hands.

The stranger stepped into the center of the room, next to the cake. "Please. I'd like my gift to be first."

The diner lapsed into a silence so complete, Mitch could swear he heard Liz's heart beating.

She looked down at her feet. Everyone was expecting her to say something. And Mitch didn't think 'thanks for the cake' was going to cut it.

"Um, everyone, I'd like you to meet Richard Beschloss. My, um, former fiancé from Boston."

Former fiancé? Mitch eyed the man again, finding he was right. He didn't like the guy. Not one bit.

At the same time, though, two other realizations materialized. Number one, the guy was alive. Number two, Liz hadn't married him.

Both made him feel as if a fifty-pound weight had been eased from his chest. They also made him feel like the biggest sucker this side of the Blue Ridge Mountains.

The rich guy cleared his throat. "Sorry to crash your party, Betsy." Mitch tensed to the point of shattering at the use of the name. "But when I found out where you were, I felt compelled to come and give you this." He held out something. It looked suspiciously like a purse.

Liz took it. "I don't know what good this is going to do me if my accounts are still frozen."

"They're not. Not as of half an hour ago." He shrugged his expensively clad shoulders. "Sorry I didn't do it sooner. I wanted an opportunity to apologize to you for my behavior in person. The only way I could do that was by limiting your resources."

"You're apologizing to me?"

Beschloss toyed with his tie. "Yes, I am. I know I was a real jerk when you said you couldn't marry me. Instead of threatening you with a lawsuit for breach of contract and assault, and freezing your accounts, I should have thanked you. You were right. We'd have only made each other miserable."

Miserable. Now that was a word. Mitch grimaced then thrust his fingers through his hair. *Miserable* about summed up what he was feeling right now.

He couldn't believe he'd gotten so worked up over something so simple. Liz had refused to marry Mr. Rich. He'd threatened her with a lawsuit. She'd decked him. Mr. Rich had frozen her accounts.

He was such a fool.

Liz silently went through her purse, then slung the strap over her shoulder. "Does this mean you dropped the assault charges?"

Mitch watched Beschloss raise his hand to his nose. "They were never officially made. Sure, I contacted the police, and they did some asking around. But Father was afraid that if I signed anything, it would be all over the tabloids the next day."

Liz bit her bottom lip in the way that drove Mitch crazy. "I guess I'm now the one who should be apologizing. I'm not usually a violent person. You must have had a hell of a time explaining that broken nose."

Down the counter from Mitch, Moses Darton elbowed his brother and snickered.

Surprisingly Beschloss chuckled. "Actually, you ended up doing me a favor. I'd broken the damn thing winter before last on the slopes of Vermont. The doctor said it never healed quite right. Your punch...well, it kind of knocked it back into place."

Liz's laugh tinkled through the diner. "Well, if you need

any help knocking anything else back into place, you let me know, huh?"

The look in Beschloss's eyes was a little too warm. A little too damn intimate. Then he bent down and kissed Liz. He lingered a little too long for Mitch's liking. He started to get up from the stool, but Bo held him back.

"It's on the cheek," Bo told him. "Just cool your heels, Mc-Coy."

Mitch forced himself to turn back to his coffee, unable to watch.

A moment later, he heard the cowbell clang again. A glance verified that Beschloss was climbing into a late-model sedan driven by the Boston P.I.

The drama over, Myra stepped forward again and shook her dark head. "Geez, woman, if that guy and Mitch are your throwaways, you're doomed to be alone forever." She thrust her gift into Liz's hands. "I don't know if this can compare to what just happened, but take it anyway."

Mitch's gaze slammed into Liz's. She blinked several times, as if trying to see his thoughts. Then Ruth patted him on the back and set a healthy helping of the chocolate cake and vanilla ice cream in front of him. His grimace deepened. They'd given him the damn halo.

"And this one's from Mitch," added Myra.

FOR THE FIRST TIME in her life, Liz didn't know what to do.

She stared at the wrapped box in front of her, then at the man whom it was from.

Ever since last night on the roof, she'd sensed a distance between herself and Mitch. A distance that had grown even more pronounced when he'd dropped her off at Gran's house. Oh, yes, he'd kissed her until her toes curled. That hadn't been the problem. That he had looked at her so seriously, almost grimly, had. And when he'd said goodbye...well, she couldn't help thinking it had been one of those forever kind of goodbyes.

Then she got the very distinct impression that he'd been avoiding her all day.

And now this.

After all his probing and prying into her life over the past ten days, she would have expected him to leap from the stool and grill Richard like a murder suspect. Instead, he just sat there looking on, as if he didn't care one way or another about the truth the unexpected encounter had revealed.

Liz sought his gaze, but found him sitting stiffly at the counter, his back to her. His odd behavior made her dread even more opening the box in front of her.

"Well, go ahead now, open it," Ruth encouraged.

Surprised to find her fingers shaking, she carefully opened the ends of the red-and-gold wrapping, no longer able to put off finding out what lay inside the box.

Her heart thudded painfully against her rib cage. What she discovered was that the item wasn't in a box at all. The box was the gift. More specifically, the sturdy, leather suitcase was. She looked up to find that Mitch had finally turned her way.

"Open it," he said quietly, the stony expression on his face warning her against following his directive.

Ezra stepped up from where he was taking bets on Lord knew what. "Yeah, open it."

Hesitantly, she unzipped the piece of luggage, holding her breath as she stared at the plain white envelope lying inside. She opened it. Inside was a fresh array of bills.

Ezra peered over her shoulder, puzzled. "It's the money he won on the bet."

Crumpling the envelope in her hands, Liz stood rooted to the spot. Unable to blink. Incapable of drawing a breath.

The reason she had thought Mitch's goodbye last night was so final was because it had been.

THE FOLLOWING MORNING Liz sat numbly on the floor of Gran's kitchen, her hands clasped tightly between her raised knees.

Gran's kitchen.

She took in the yellowing walls, the outdated appliances, the chipped linoleum floor. That's exactly what this place was, and would always be: Gran's house. A place where she had spent her summers. A collection of rooms chock-full of memories. While it had been the only constant during her otherwise unsettled life, the neglected old house had never been home.

Liz forced herself up from the floor and crossed to where all her belongings were neatly stacked on the narrow counter. Belongings that included the precious few things she'd collected when she was younger but had never taken away because she had always thought the place would be there.

She fingered a faded blue ribbon she'd won in a spelling bee at the Manchester County Fair when she was twelve.

Her heart expanded and tears flooded her eyes. Mitch was right. She needed to sell the house. To finally close the door on a past that was better off forgotten. Especially now that she knew Manchester no longer held anything for her.

Scanning the barren room, she picked up the suitcase Mitch had given her and began piling the few clothes she'd bought inside.

She didn't know what, exactly, had happened with Mitch. One minute everything was perfect, then the next...

The next he acted as though none of it mattered.

Could it be as she suspected after their first time together at the diner? That his intention all along had been to get what he couldn't have seven years ago? She tightly closed her eyes, thinking about how willing a participant she'd been. She honestly didn't think the words *casual sex* were part of his vocabulary. After all, he'd waited how long before their wedding night?

A night that had never come.

She bit down hard on her bottom lip. She supposed that maybe this was exactly what she deserved for having done what she had so long ago.

She slowly pushed her hair back from her face, and swiped at an errant tear. At a couple of weak points during the day, she had hoped Mitch would come ambling through the back door, that endearing mischievous grin on his face. Give her a cocky "Well, how did that feel, Liz?" Then she would whack him and forgive all. It was the only reason she had stayed through the morning rather than waiting at Dulles airport for the first flight out to Atlanta. But his crushing absence from her doorstep told her it wasn't going to happen. He had meant what he said, and the only thing left for her to do was leave.

She laughed caustically and folded the top of the bag. Who was it who had said Manchester was but a pit stop on her way to another city? Was that her? Not that she noticed that person anymore. She now knew that the instant she'd run into Mitch on that deserted road, she had reached her final destination.

Taking one last look around the kitchen to make certain everything was in order for the Realtor she planned to contact, she grabbed the bag and stepped toward the mudroom. The setting sun slanted through the open door, shining a spotlight on one of the red shoes she had worn into town.

She reached over and plucked it up off the floor, unable to locate the other. It occurred to her that the shoes were her running shoes. No sneakers for her. When she left some place behind, she did it in style. She should have known the instant she traded her white satin pumps for her red shoes the morning she was supposed to marry Richard that she wasn't going to exchange wedding or any other vows that day. She stared down at her beige macramé sandals that matched her tan skirt and blouse and frowned. She was ruining her image. At any rate, she was tired of moving around. Come what may, the instant her plane touched down in Atlanta, her feet would never leave the ground again. Emotionally as well as physically.

Tugging the door closed and stashing the key on the nearby window ledge, she headed toward her Pacer, tossing the lone shoe into an empty trash can as she passed.

15

COULD THINGS get any worse?

Liz stood in front of the baggage-claim conveyor belt, then looked at her watch. There was no way in the world a puddle-jumping flight from D.C. to Atlanta should have taken so long. But, as the pilot had informed them when they started to make their descent into the southern capital, due to a violent line of thunderstorms, their plane had been re-routed...through Detroit. *Detroit*, for crying out loud. A destination two hours in the other direction. Tack onto that the one-hour take-off pattern after they had landed, and another two to make it back to Atlanta, and she was suffering from a major case of airplane sickness. Not the kind that required a small paper bag, but that necessitated getting far, and fast, from any and all airports.

Heaving a hefty sigh, Liz watched the same luggage make the rounds again, hers nowhere to be found. When she'd left Virginia, the sun had been shining....

For the tenth time in as many minutes, she found herself wondering what Mitch was doing. And for the tenth time she ordered herself to stop it. She didn't care if he was at the diner chatting it up with Bo and Ruth. Or home with his father and whichever brother or brothers had decided to drop in. She didn't want to think of him feeding his mismatched menagerie of animals, or throwing fresh straw in the stalls in preparation for the thoroughbreds he'd soon be breeding there. Or how much she would like to breed with him. In fact, she didn't want to think about him at all.

Liar.

All she yearned to do was think about Mitch. She wanted to check into a hotel room, put the Do Not Disturb sign on the door, order up everything room service had to offer, raid the mini bar and pretend clocks didn't exist until the acute ache in her heart began to ease. Only she thought that the ache might never ease. She didn't have enough resources for never. But she could swing a good month if she had to.

She finally spotted what she thought was her suitcase being spit out by the luggage monster. As the bag slowly made its way toward her, she hoped the limo service had been able to arrange for someone to meet her. "Can't promise anything," they'd told her. "Seems everyone and their brother wants a limo today, what with the concert and all." She hadn't bothered to ask what concert.

She eyed her new suitcase. It was so battered, she questioned ownership, and almost didn't reach out in time to grab it. A man helped her, mumbling something about stupid females in response to her thank you. She ignored him and hurried for the door.

Through the crush of people, she searched for the white sign with her name on it. Please let them have sent someone. She really didn't feel up to waiting for a taxi in the rain. Then again, if it got any wetter, she could just float to her hotel.

Someone bumped into her from behind, forcing her into the person ahead of her. Her breath rushed from her in a sharp whoosh and her suitcase slid from her grasp. She watched in paralyzed horror as it skidded across the marble tile, thunked down onto its side then sprang open.

At the same time, she spotted the sign with her name on it. Good, someone had made...

She froze. Slowly she read the sign a second time. Elizabeth/Betsy/Liz Braden was written across it crookedly in black marker.

Her heart skipped a beat. Then another. But she couldn't seem to take her gaze from that sign, even when the person holding it lowered it to hip level.

She moaned aloud. She'd recognize those jeans-clad hips anywhere.

Mitch.

Mitch shifted his weight from one boot to the other. *Come on, Liz, look at me, damn it. I have to know my coming here isn't another in a long line of major mistakes.*

She had yet to lift her gaze to his face.

He squared his shoulders and stood a little straighter. Mistake or no, he wasn't going anywhere. He'd camp out on her doorstep if he had to, he didn't care. Because sometime between last night and this afternoon, he'd realized he hadn't been a fool for loving her. He'd been a fool for never letting her know how much he loved her. How much he needed her in his life.

Of course, the realization had come after Pops had practically shouted, "You did *what?*" at him when he told the old man what had happened. Then Sean had let him in on exactly how he'd misread his advice two nights before. When he'd said he should be prepared to live with the consequences, he'd meant *after* he'd told Liz exactly how he felt. And didn't it just beat all that he was sitting back like a dumb fool as the love of his life left town...again.

Of course, he'd only felt lousier after the talking down. And it had taken him a whole hour of pounding fence posts into the ground a mile away from the house before he figured everything out.

Liz hadn't had to come back to Manchester...she'd *chosen* to.

Even though Liz's accounts had been frozen until yesterday, she'd had the resources to leave town after selling her Lexus...but *hadn't*.

Liz hadn't said she didn't love him, he had *assumed* she didn't...even though every gut instinct he'd ever had told him differently.

And when Liz had said "sex like that is almost enough to keep me here," that hadn't meant she was leaving. It had meant she was waiting for him to offer her another reason to stay.

And, like an idiot, he'd instead given her every reason to leave.

He bit back a curse. Damn him and his stupid pride. He'd been so afraid of history repeating itself that he'd basically guaranteed that it would.

Finally, Liz's gaze moved up his torso, lingered on his neck, then shifted to his face. She looked like she'd been through hell and back. And she'd never looked so damn beautiful.

He gave her the biggest grin ever, dropped the sign and held out his arms. She catapulted toward him so fast, she got her shoe caught in her open suitcase and he had to catch her before she hit the hard tile headfirst.

She stood back to look in his face. "How did you know where I was? How did you get here before me?" She waved her hand in the air. "Forget the second question. You probably could have driven here faster. Just answer the first."

He slid the brochure he'd taken from her wall from his pocket and put it in her hand. "Remember this?"

She sighed and flung herself into his arms again.

He held her so tightly he was afraid he'd snap her in two. "Lord, woman, do you have any idea how much I love you?"

Liz kissed him. On the mouth. On the chin. On the brow. "Not half as much as I love you, McCoy." She drew back and slugged him in the arm. "Now what in the hell took you so long?"

He chuckled. She hit him again. He grasped her wrists and hauled her until she was flush against him. "Know of any good hotels in this town?"

Her eyes narrowed even as she ran that naughty little tongue of hers across her lips.

"A hotel with a grade-A jeweler in the lobby?" he added.

She didn't say anything for the longest time. Then a smile slowly spread across her face. "Ask me, Mitch."

He cleared his throat. "Should I get down on one knee?"

She struggled against his hold, presumably to hit him again.

"All right, all right." He planted his boots solidly on the floor. Gave his head a toss to loosen the kinks in his neck. Then he gazed deep into her eyes. Eyes he hoped he'd be looking into for the rest of his life. "Will you marry me, Elizabeth/Betsy/Liz Braden?"

She kissed him so hard, so thoroughly, he wanted to tug her into the nearest men's room and have his way with her in one of the stalls.

"Yes, Mitch McCoy, I'll marry you."

He gathered her close and took a deep breath of her sweet-smelling hair. It was then another realization dawned. The excitement he'd been seeking in his life could never be found in any job. That's why he'd quit the FBI, retired from private investigating. And he knew now he wouldn't have found it in horse-breeding, either. Liz was the only one who could provide the kind of excitement he was looking for. The only one capable of keeping him guessing, keeping him running, keeping him attuned to what life and love were truly all about.

"Does this mean we can go home now?" she asked.

He swept a damp tendril of hair back from her face. "Yes, angel, it does."

_____Epilogue_____

WHAT A DIFFERENCE three weeks makes.

Mitch stood at the end of the aisle, tugging at his bow tie. Jake stood next to him, once again playing the role of best man. Every chapel pew was filled to capacity, the occupants, decked out in their Sunday best, waving fans or songbooks to combat the heat. He was somewhat relieved that he wasn't the only one who felt like he was on a hot plate. But the sweat dotting the back of his neck had very little to do with the fact that the small chapel wasn't air-conditioned.

Could it be that he'd suddenly developed a case of stage fright? He realized his uneasiness had very little to do with standing up in front of a crowd, really. What made him feel like rushing for the door and hurling behind the nearest bush was being in front of _this_ crowd, prepared to marry the _same_ woman...and being scared to death that the same damn thing would happen all over again.

He nearly groaned.

Pops motioned to him from the front pew, indicating his tie was crooked. Mitch toyed with the stiff material until Sean nodded.

God, everything about this day eerily mirrored that life-altering day seven years ago. Even the townsfolk seemed to be sitting in the exact same spots they had been back then. Liz's mother Sunny sat up front and center on the bride's side, looking more like Liz's sister than her mother in her crinkled skirt and tank top. The Darton brothers fidgeted in what had to be the same brown suits near the back of the chapel. Ruth sat smiling at him from the bride's side. Ezra poked someone in front of him, likely hammering out the details of his latest betting pool. Even Josiah stood quietly in the back, having relinquished his rocking chair in front of the general store for the day.

Then there was his family, the McCoys.

Aside from Jake, who stood next to him, they sat in the front right pew. He caught Pops's gaze and swallowed so hard the old man must have heard it, because his grin widened. He still hadn't found out exactly who Sean McCoy was dating, none of his brothers had, but they weren't going to stop until they came up with a name.

Connor sat to Pops's right, his attention more on his watch than the events around him. Mitch glanced at his own watch, the heat factor vaulting higher as he realized they were already running ten minutes late.

Despite his initial attempt to laugh it off at the house, Connor was the one who took the news of Pops's secretive, apparently serious, dating the hardest and let Pops and everyone know it. Before the ceremony, he'd heartily slapped Mitch on the back and offered his condolences. Despite his anxiety, Mitch cracked a smile. Leave it to Connor to equate marriage with death. Out of the five of them, Connor seemed to be the one who took seriously their childhood vow never to marry.

His gaze slid to Jake, and he amended his assessment. Jake took everything way too seriously. Tall and sober, he was the only one who looked comfortable in the monkey suit he wore. Not surprising. If it was confining and required rules to work, wear or eat it, then Jake was right at home. At one point, dyed-in-the-wool Trekkie Marc had nicknamed him Spock. But it hadn't stuck. Could have had something to do with the chokehold Jake had put on him. It wasn't so much the physical act that had nipped the name-calling in the bud. It was the calm way Jake had done it: one minute he'd been passing Marc in the hall, the next Marc had virtually been part of the wall.

Next came David, who elbowed Connor in the ribs and whispered something. Connor gave him a threatening look and David laughed. Mitch guessed being the youngest gave David much of his cocky confidence. They all took more guff from him than they'd ever taken from one another. As he looked at the great-looking blond kid—kid? Sheesh, he had to be pushing thirty—he sometimes wondered if they'd all been raised in the same household. It was more than the physical characteristics that made them different. Where he and the others had always been cautious in their relations with women, David had pretty much compensated by dating so many women they had stopped trying to keep track of their names long ago. Then again, his youngest brother's approach might be different, but it ultimately found him in the same spot as Connor and Jake—unmarried.

His gaze fell on Marc. Some of the tension melted from his shoulders. Where everything else was essentially the same as seven years ago, here was a palpable difference. Go figure. Marc was not only married, he was due to be a daddy in a few short months. And while his and Melanie's honeymoon had been a disaster, all one had to do was watch them watching each other to know that those two had the stuff it took to make it.

The first opening strains of organ music snapped his attention away from his family and back to the unbearably long aisle in the small chapel. He slipped a finger under his bow tie and tugged, then felt it to make sure it was still straight. Myra's wiry form filled the doorway, festooned in purple satin from head to toe. Mitch didn't know if it was just him, but Myra seemed determined to take an inordinate amount of time stepping down the flower-strewn aisle. *Baby steps*, he thought. She was taking baby steps. If he didn't know better, he'd think she was deliberately trying to delay things....

Behind her, Bo came into view. Mitch nearly slumped in relief at the appearance of the short, beefy cook. With no male family members of her own, Liz had again asked the gregarious Bo to give her away. A role Bo readily agreed to play.

Finally, Myra stood across from him and the organist began pounding out the "Wedding March."

Mitch's heart skipped one beat, two, then beat so loudly, he could hear nothing but its throbbing tattoo. Bo looked behind him, then quickly to his left. When he turned to face the chapel again, a panicked expression creased his aging face. Mitch's stomach bottomed out.

Oh, God, she's going to do it again.

Sensing that something was amiss, a low murmur began among the guests. A hum that mimicked the ringing in Mitch's head. Out of the corner of his eye, he saw Connor begin to get up, then Pops slap a hand on his arm. Bo disappeared from the door and the din in the chapel grew to a noisy roar. Even the organist stopped playing.

A sudden, suffocating silence settled over the room as, one by one, the guests turned their solemn eyes to him.

The past was playing itself out all over again. His feet seemed cemented to the spot up to his knees. His body eerily frozen. He could do nothing but stare at the spot where his bride should have appeared ten minutes ago. Nothing....

Then came the unmistakable rustle of fabric.

"Aw, Lizzie, you're going to rip the damn thing." Bo's voice wafted down the aisle.

Everyone snapped their attention back to the still-empty doorway. Mitch's gaze had never moved.

"To hell with the dress, Bo, I've got a groom to marry."

Then, suddenly, all that was Liz filled the doorway. Yards upon yards of puffy white fabric swirled around her figure, hugging her in all the right places. Mitch blinked once, twice, certain he was seeing things. Then Liz nearly fell to the side before Bo steadied her. It was then that Mitch noticed she was tugging on her skirt. A loud ripping rent the air, finally freeing the material from where it was caught on the heel of her right shoe. Ah, but they just weren't any old shoes. Mitch felt a grin begin to edge across his face when he spotted the purple skyscrapers that came into view as she grabbed her skirt in both hands and lifted the material free.

His gaze slammed into hers. She was flushed, but the sparkle in her hazel eyes nearly knocked him over. Before the organist could even resume playing, she started toward him, her step quickening the closer she got, until she was at nearly a full run by the time she crashed into him.

Mitch caught her shoulders to steady her, his fingers digging into her soft flesh beneath the ruined dress.

"Sorry I'm late. I ran into, um, some problems." Her voice was breathless and emotion-filled. Mitch's heart again skipped a beat. But this time it was for all the right reasons.

"I was afraid...I mean, I thought..."

She laid a white-gloved finger against his lips. "Shh."

The pastor cleared his throat. "Ladies and gentlemen, we are gathered here today—"

When Mitch hauled Liz against his chest, a collective gasp filled the chapel, along with a few awkward chuckles. "What say we get this over with, angel? Say 'I will.'"

Liz blinked at him several times. Then realization dawned on her sweet face. She smiled. "I will."

"Me, too." Together they pushed and tugged and pulled until her veil was lifted and lay askew on her head. Then he did what he hadn't been able to wait to do: he kissed her. Truly, madly, deeply kissed her. His intention was to make those toes of hers curl inside those purple things she called shoes.

EZRA'S TRIUMPHANT SHOUT filled the otherwise silent chapel, followed by low groans. Liz reluctantly allowed Mitch to tug his mouth away from hers, welcoming his quick nip after he pulled away.

"All right everybody, pay up," Ezra said, racing around the chapel and snatching the bills nearly everyone pulled from their pockets.

Liz blinked. "What's going on?"

Mitch tightened his arms around her, his nearness warming her. "I don't know, but somehow I think our bet wasn't the only one going on around here."

Ezra hooted and counted out some of his winnings, handing a portion to Ruth. "Mitch, my dear boy, you're darn right there was another bet going. It started the moment you ran into Liz on that dark road." He grinned and hugged Ruth to his side. "This fine lady here and I started the wager that you two—" he shook a finger at them "—would end up married yet."

Mitch chuckled and buried his face in Liz's neck.

"Liz?" he murmured.

She entangled her fingers in his soft hair. "What?"

"I need you to do me a favor." He glanced up at her, his gaze serious. "I need you to get rid of that damn suitcase I gave you. 'Cause angel, you won't be needing it anymore."

Her laugh mingled with the boisterous conversation swirling around them.

Oh, yes, this was definitely different from what had happened seven years ago, Mitch thought. And he liked this much, much better.

There was no escaping it. He was, and always would be, the spy, P.I.... Oh, hell, just the plain old guy who loved her.

HEART OF THE WEST

Every Man Has His Price!

Lost Springs Ranch was famous for turning young mavericks into good men. So word that the ranch was in financial trouble sent a herd of loyal bachelors stampeding back to Wyoming to put themselves on the auction block!

HARLEQUIN®
Makes any time special ™

Visit us at www.romance.net

PHHOWGEN

Mother's Day is Around the Corner...
Give the gift that celebrates Life and Love!

Show Mom you care by presenting her with a one-year subscription to:

HARLEQUIN
WORLD'S BEST
Romances

For only $4.96—
That's **75% off the cover price.**

This easy-to-carry, compact magazine delivers 4 exciting romance stories by some of the very best romance authors in the world.

Plus each issue features personal moments with the authors, author biographies, a crossword puzzle and more...

A one-year subscription includes 6 issues full of love, romance and excitement to warm the heart.

To send a gift subscription, write the recipient's name and address on the coupon below, enclose a check for $4.96 and mail it today. In a few weeks, we will send you an acknowledgment letter and a special postcard so you can notify this lucky person that a fabulous gift is on the way!

Yes! I would like to purchase a one-year gift subscription (that's 6 issues) of WORLD'S BEST ROMANCES, for only $4.96. I save over 75% off the cover price of $21.00.   MRGIFT00

This is a special gift for:

Name _____

Address _____ Apt# _____

City _____ State _____ Zip _____

From _____

Address _____ Apt# _____

City _____ State _____ Zip _____

Mail to: HARLEQUIN WORLD'S BEST ROMANCES
P.O. Box 37254, Boone, Iowa, 50037-0254 Offer valid in the U.S. only.